# Nfr IWN

## THE CITY OF THE SUN

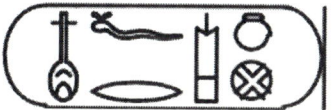

# ALY BRISHA

Nfr IWN | The City of the Sun
Copyright 2015 by Aly Brisha

All rights reserved. No part of this book may be used or reproduced in any matter without prior written permission.

ISBNs
Softcover: 978-1-988186-34-4
eBook: 978-1-988186-35-1

Printed in Canada

# Nfr IWN

## The City of the Sun

The work ritual of Dr. Gamal Omran in his second floor apartment at Al Dokee district in Cairo hadn't changed in 35 years. Each day began with the aroma of a traditional Arabic coffee flavoured with exotic fragrant spices, which Dr. G prepared himself. The sound of classical music flowed forth, encompassing every corner of this empty apartment which had never been inhabited by wife nor child. Dr. G certainly deserved the title that all of his colleagues had given him: "The Monk of Science". His apartment, which consisted of only two rooms - one for sleeping and the other an office - fit the title appropriately. This living space resembled more the quarters of a humble monk who had no interest in the glamour of the world, rather than an esteemed/accomplished professor. No one would believe that this was in fact the home of a great thinker who had received the highest prize of the Egyptian state for Arts; this was the home of a man who had been knighted by the Queen of England in appreciation of his achievement and research in the human sciences.

On this hot August night Dr. G was carrying a cup of coffee on a handmade copper tray through the corridor toward the office where he would submerge himself in his papers and books to continue the study that had absorbed the last five years of his life. Yet on this particular night his academic mind was not as clear as he found himself closing his eyes just as the famous Korsakov symphony *Scheherazade* was drawing to a close. He motioned with his hands as if he was a violinist recounting this timeless legend. Suddenly, the obtrusive smell of dank, heavy tobacco entered the space aggressively, causing him to tremble while he stared toward the dark corner of the room.

Dr. G didn't realize exactly what was happening. He saw the blue haze of smoke before he felt an enormous surge through his body, one so great he fell to the floor in a state of great paralysis. He was conscious but his body could not respond to his brain's signals. He saw the approaching shoes of the intruder and felt the claws of his attacker flip him over onto his back. The smell of the smoke grew denser as the thin face of a man appeared in front of him; between his teeth he gripped a cigar with a ferocious smile. Dr. G. felt a strong grasp on the back of his neck and a strong surge of pain on his jaw; his mouth automatically opened in response and then he felt a light sting on the roof of his mouth. His consciousness began to melt away in a light fog, growing deeper and deeper until there was nothing but darkness. Before his soul left his body he could hear the sound of his murderer hissing like a viper.

*********

The night shift schedule at the journalistic institution of "THE SPHINX" was known by almost all of the 1700 journalists and employees who worked there. They were proud to adhere to the very minute - even second - of this schedule that was rooted in 130 years of tradition ever since the Syrian refugee "Elias Khouri" had founded the institution in Cairo after escaping with his family from the ethnic massacres that had taken place in the mountains of Lebanon. Khouri had founded "THE SPHINX" in 1878 which had since become the biggest institution in the Middle East. Even when the Germans bombarded the old building during WW2, the shift system was still ongoing and never broken. On the day of bombardment the third edition of the journal wasn't delayed even by one minute - even though the raids of the Desert Fox were specifically targeting the building, it being the source of English propaganda in Egypt. Although the raids managed to destroy the journal's print house, the chairman of publishing insisted that there be no delay in the journal's latest edition. In his determination he used an old stone press printing machine that had been used to print pamphlets for nightclubs and theatres found in the downtown of the city at the turn of the 20th century. Thus, that particular edition of the journal came out in small pieces on ballots. The institute still had the originals in the main corridors of the new building. This building had come into existence after the "Egyptian Army's coup". This history was described in the red-coloured header of the front page of the journal on the 24th of July, 1952 and was still preserved behind glass in a show window in the same corridor.

The second edition of the journal was always carried out at midnight. Photographers and editors of the respective departments of crime, foreign policy, politics, and linguistics had to stay on the premises, as did the editor of the main board. The duty of this group was to remain on standby overnight, ready for anything that might happen. This was a pretty old system, or as some called it: an unwritten holy ritual. Nobody had ever had the nerve to change any of these details for over 80 years. But Mariam Gatas, the photojournalist, knew that her presence at this late hour violated another sacred ritual in the institution, which was the impossibility of a female joining the team on the overnight shift.

Mariam Gatas had finally achieved this special privilege after a long fight which had lasted the entire nine months she had been at the institution. In the first weeks she had felt like her dignity was stabbed when Mr. Zakaria, the old head of the photography department, had scheduled the shifts of the on-staff photojournalists and she had overheard some sarcastic comments from her colleagues regarding her being excluded from the midnight shift. Instead, her skills were to be allotted only for specific themes such as art and literature news, far apart from real reporting and crime. When she had asked the head of the department about this scheduling, he said it was all well-intended. This was following tradition, and after all she was the first female photojournalist on staff. The message given to her was that she should be happy to be the exception. The general rule of Egyptian journalism was to never recognize a female photojournalist, although even the position of head editor had been occasionally occupied by a female since the early 1920s. Photojournalism, as an early profession for females, was almost empty of the female component. This was true for a woman like

Mariam, even bearing in mind her experience of covering three wars during her career with three famous American news agencies.

With assertion, Mariam challenged all of the traditions and rules of her family. She never gave up in her declared war against which she found barriers that could have restricted her from having the free will to choose for herself the way her life could be. Mariam had been brought up and educated in an American style, meaning that she always wanted to challenge the part of herself that belonged to the conservative south Egyptian way of thinking.

She had always insisted on working extra hours, and stayed long after her shift was already done. Every night she stayed working during the night shift, which was exclusively a shift for males. However, she never cared about that silly rule. As well, she always wore blue jeans instead of a skirt.

Night shift tended to make the men more careless about their words, the language they used, and the kind of jokes they told. However, seeing Mariam amongst them made them restless. From time to time they would sneak a quick look at her legs or other parts of her body.

She found it very insulting to hear her workmates laughing about something but once she approached them they would all of a sudden stop laughing. Sometimes she would hear them tell jokes that were inappropriate for a lady to hear. Disregarding her presence, her coworkers would exchange those kind of male jokes that would never be said in public. She would then play dumb and pretend that she never heard a word

By taking advantage of the fact she had been raised in the States, the language would at times provide a great shelter from embarrassment. So even if somebody tried to translate to her what was said, the joke would lose its joy in the translation.

When one of the city's biggest condos collapsed on the first day of the Muslim feast Al-Adha, Mariam was the only one who got the story, as she had been the first one on the scene. At that point her colleagues surrendered to her becoming a nonofficial member of the night team. They had tried to take advantage of her proactive efforts, but the collapsing of the building had surprised both them and her. All of the international news agencies had used her photographs from that night, and she had finally received recognition from the chief of editing. He had awarded her the privilege of being the first female allowed to join the overnight team one night a week.

On this particular night Mariam was not so happy for this privilege she had been granted after so long of a fight. She left the building at three a.m. in a black car that was inscribed with the institution's emblem: the face of a Sphinx wearing a mysterious look and a smashed nose. In the backseat beside her sat Isaak Shoaib, her colleague from the crime department who also worked nights. It was an unseasonably cold night for December, a night where the rains never ceased with the rare exception of only a few moments.

"Please Hussein, drive carefully so we can get back safe," Isaak raised his voice, talking to the driver. Then leaning against her comically he commented, "He has to pay attention, because if something happens to us the accident wouldn't find anyone to shoot it and the story wouldn't make the third edition."

Mariam forced herself to smile and exchange with him a few sentences about the nature of the mission that they were about to carry out. Then she turned away.

Following the movement of the car going through the streets of downtown Cairo heading east, the road was totally deserted except for small puddles of water that diverted their direct path to the desired destination. The driver had to swerve towards New Cairo. This district had borne the features of the European style of design since the Belgium "Édouard, Baron Empain" had founded it at the turn of the 20th century. The car headed left towards the district of "Ain Shams". By the dim lights of the road appeared clusters of the falling rain. The sidewalks and streets had started to vanish along with the aristocratic memories of Baron Empain to be substituted by late 20th century ugly random buildings that were forming the western part of the poverty-stricken district of Ain Shams. As in the beginning of the 20th century, Cairo was expanding in a quiet, planned, rational way at the hands of people like Baron. By the end of the 20th century Cairo had become an ugly city that had expanded as the population bomb had exploded in a way that made it appear random like rubble from a bomb thrown every which way from the city's centre.

When the car reached the bottom of the bridge, the sound of a splash rose above the sound of the pouring rain. A fountain covered the car as it drove through a pool of accumulated rain water. As they left the centre of Cairo, the features diminished and they began to enter a place of poor houses and narrow streets covered by a thick layer of garbage, mud, and sewage water. The rain water had started to diminish until it was nothing but a drizzle or mist.

When the car stopped at one of the alleyways, it wasn't hard to recognize that they had arrived at the site of the accident as the flashing lights of the siren split the darkness into the two colours of red and blue.

Gathered around the accident were lots of policemen, curious passersby, workers, and digging machines. The journalists exited the car and walked towards the blue and red lights.

*\*\*\*\*\*\*\*\*\**

On the other side of the Atlantic Ocean, although the Blackberry was ringing continuously, it wasn't attracting the attention of anyone in the

Historical Studies Academy (HSA) of Massachusetts' largest conference hall. And when Professor John Howard finally looked at the illuminated screen, he raised his eyebrows in surprise after calculating the time difference and realizing it was three a.m. in Cairo. He smiled lightly as he discretely looked down at the screen. "Our friend is either very devoted to his job or he is insane staying up this late," he thought to himself as he opened the message. After reading the first line, he realized his friend was neither insane nor overly devoted but was rather raising the alert of a huge catastrophe. Action needed to be taken immediately. After less than five minutes, Professor Howard withdrew rapidly from the conference hall as his finger tapped away on the keypad. He had to make lots of urgent phone calls across the Atlantic.

*********

If journalism is the job of looking for trouble, then a policeman's job is one and the same. The relationship between these two jobs is ruled by a sacred code that differs from one country to another. In Britain the dealing between these two sides is automatic; it is governed by a strict coldness but at the same time decency. In America there is a feeling of anxiety which covers this relationship. The tension can be seen in the ironic way a policeman deals with a journalist while eating a donut or chewing gum. The policeman spreads his power over the journalist while remaining cognizant of the limits and regulations of laws that tie up his power. In many Arab Gulf countries the policeman tries to be decent but at the same time he makes great efforts to hide his real feelings of suspicion towards journalists. For him these efforts are just enough to put barriers in the journalists' way by referring everything to his superiors.

But in Egypt the policeman holds the journalist in high esteem, calling him 'Pasha' which means Lord. The policeman in Egypt forces the journalist to respond at the same professional level while he practices dealing the game of power and control through his speech. He insists on appearing in control and he acts as though he is doing the journalist a great favour, a favour which depends on the way the journalist deals with him. In the policeman's mind, one hand washes the other. He is also keen to show by very rapidly spoken sentences some clues of his high class in literature and knowledge just to demonstrate that he is on the same level and understands politics, culture, and the ability to read between the lines. And within this bubble of control the policeman is keen for fortification. He is very happy, like a child, when a journalist promises to use his name or his picture in a statement alongside the same news that he is there to report. Actually, it is precisely this lack of clear regulations regarding the balance of power which rules the relationship between them. The journalist knows that the cop can hinder his work by obstructing his ease in getting the news. Also, the cop could go to the extreme and practice violations against the journalist. On the other hand, the cop knows that the journalist, when he is able, could bite him like a viper. And this is a very painful bite, either because of his social networks, which might be bigger than what the officer might expect, or because of his ability to include some negative details in the reporting that could show the cop in a bad light. This could be enough for the policeman to be blamed by his superiors.

Thus, there are special rituals practiced by journalists in dealing with cops in Egypt. Those rituals are learned by the journalists in the crime department faster than anyone else. Isaak Shoaib was very knowledgeable in these rituals of dealing with cops, as he quickly explained to Mariam in fast words while they were walking out of the car. She was to let him do the talking and not interfere unless she was needed.

Of the two officers who were sitting in the police car, one was a young lieutenant and the other was elder but lower in rank. The right hand of the senior officer was holding a walkie-talkie that never stopped chattering. They were sitting in the car in complete laziness, feigning immunity to the feminine beauty that stood before them.

"Good evening, Pasha," said Isaak, addressing the young lieutenant.

"Welcome, journalist."

"It's awful weather tonight, but fortunately the rain has stopped."

"What brings you over here in such awful weather? You'd be better off staying home in your warm bed. But it's early bird gets the worm with you, am I right?"

Isaak knew very well how to handle this point in any conversation with any policeman. When a policeman started speaking about getting the news first and referred to the circumstances of his work, he needed to use a tone of appreciation. He needed to convey pity for the sacrifices of the devoted policeman to his work. That is why Isaak answered by saying,

"God help you and bless your heart, Pasha; it's enough suffering for you that you are waiting out here on this cold and dark night all in the name of your duty."

The young lieutenant got out of his car and offered Isaak a cigarette. He offered another one to Mariam which she refused politely. The three of them walked together towards the site of the accident. The ground was muddy and bumpy and the digging machines were encircling the wreckage. A big sign bore the name of a large contracting company which was carrying out this digging to extend the district's sewage line. Mariam immediately took out her camera and started snapping away. The young lieutenant smiled broadly when he saw that she was keen to take his picture from different angles. He was explaining to Isaak how during digging the workers had discovered a large monumental stone buried seven metres deep. At this point the policeman had been informed of their discovery. The young man was keen on giving the names of his superiors to be mentioned in the report.

When they approached the discovery site, they saw a big rectangular hole extending underneath one of the houses with a length exceeding ten metres, a width of over four metres, and a depth so deep that nobody could see the bottom. Its walls were protected by strong wooden supports. Mariam stared into the darkness of the hole. Though she tried to use her flash, the light failed to overcome the dense darkness beneath. With much worry the young lieutenant was watching her as she tested the wooden supports and tied up her gear bag on her back. She was getting ready to descend into the passage.

"Where the hell are you going?"

"It's impossible to shoot from here. I have to get down there in order to see the stone well," she said as she bent a small lamp around her head like those used by mineworkers. Her bag was full of everything she needed like something MacGyver might have. Her colleague smiled when he saw her personal items which indeed fit her nickname of The Girl Scout. All of her workmates had taken to calling her this as she was constantly saying "Always be ready."

But the young lieutenant yelled at her: "It's not an easy matter; that is a difficult climb and it is probably very dangerous."

Isaak laughed out loud while trying to calm the young lieutenant down.

He whispered in his ear words that Mariam could not hear: "Let her be. She is stubborn. Trust me, she will probably return after two metres of complete darkness."

※※※※※※※※※※

The American State of Massachusetts held the title of being the World's Capital of Science and Education. With over 500 universities and colleges, the most famous of all were Harvard and the highly esteemed MIT. From those two institutes, 146 individuals had received the Nobel Prize. Yet the state had no more than twelve votes in the electoral congress, which was why the Americans considered Massachusetts to be a middle class state as it held very little political sway. California exceeded Massachusetts with 55 votes, and even states such as Pennsylvania, Florida, and Ohio excelled by always playing a crucial role in choosing the next President of the United States. In spite of all this, Massachusetts held an intangible ranking in the great American electoral marathon as it was considered the scientific and academic capital of a nation that valued science and technology most important in its basis. That is why it was not a coincidence that seven of the American presidents had graduated from one university among the many existing in Massachusetts, with the most important of these presidents being John F. Kennedy and Franklin D. Roosevelt. Even though the hot race of the presidential election in America was just a few months away, the identity of the opposing presidential candidate had not yet been released. HSA's annual celebration had begun as if it was a very early trial session of the real upcoming election. In addition to the existence of the American president who was preparing to defend his position in a few months for a new term, there were too many candidates from the opposing party; more than one senator from congress; heads of national security, foreign affairs, and defence in congress; in addition to the heads of the most popular American Ivy League universities. All the politicians were trying hard to garner the support of these universities on their respective sides as they were considered the most capable of organizing campaigns or fundraising to support candidates.

For Jonas Krux, the head reporter of Daily Boston, there was something surprising in this celebration. He had covered such celebrations for over 45 years, and so he knew that all of the friendly chatter and cocktail talk between the elite that appeared like hugs and kisses between the leaders of the Middle East were fake. These were usually exchanged in front of the media people while they held daggers behind their backs poised ready to stab.

"Don't be overwhelmed or surprised, because this will hinder you from understanding that the reality of these celebrations is the opposite of what these people are saying."

This was how Mr. Krux had advised his younger colleagues in how to approach their first time covering such a large event. But on that particular night old Jonas could not stop himself from experiencing the weird feeling of surprise and incomprehension at the absence of Professor John Howard, the Executive Manager of HSA.

"A health problem hinders John Howard from attending. But that's nonsense. My knowledge of the professor would dictate that even if he was dead he would have ordered the undertaker to bring his coffin to the ceremony," thought Jonas to himself, while he questioned the real reason for the man's failure to attend. "There must be a very interesting reason for this."

But Jonas's surprise and suspicion would have been doubled if he had known that John Howard at that very moment wasn't technically absent from the ceremony. Only a few metres away from the main hall, the man was hiding from the President of the United States and a bunch of very important guests as he sat before his computer screen sending numerous emails and communications throughout the world. The destiny of the world he knew and the world which he was keen to keep would be decided in the next few hours.

*************

After Mariam grabbed hold of the wooden support, she hung her body over the pit and threw her legs in the air as delicately as a leopardess winning a black belt in karate to reach what looked like a primitive wooden ladder. Descending was easy somehow because the supports were strong and stable, but the problem was that the rain had made the wood a bit wet and slippery. The walls of the hole appeared to be saturated with water and therefore weak, warning Mariam of an impending danger. She was scared that the ladder would collapse under her weight. And when she reached the depth of three metres she found herself engulfed in darkness. She touched the lamp attached to her head to throw dim lighting around the cold place. The light was hardly enough to see where to put her feet while she manoeuvred from one support to another. As she descended she carried on cursing in English, because it was getting harder and harder the lower she went. All of her clothes were covered in mud from the forced contact between her body and the wooden supports. When she finally hit the muddy ground, she found pieces of stone that the workers had laid down to move around on. The bottom of the pit was covered by a layer of water of about 30 centimetres. She moved around first to her right and then to her left before she found the artefact.

"Oh my god, it's a really beautiful thing!" Mariam raised her voice in English while staring at the stone which was about two feet from where she had hit the ground after her descent. With a height of about 70 centimetres from the ground and a width of about 20 centimetres, the stone was rectangular like a big pink granite block. The upper part of the stone was about one-and-a-half metres in width, but it appeared that the major part of the stone was still submerged under the earth. On the visible part of the stone there were three lines of hieroglyphics. At the bottom there was a big relief of the familiar Egyptian symbol of life. Beside it was another weird symbol which caused Mariam to immediately feel that she had seen it before. Quickly she brought out her camera, loaded it with a highly sensitive Kodak film (ISO 800), locked up the flash, and used a wide angle lens. She then turned on the cold fluorescents from her bag and used them to sidelight the stone. The shooting took her five minutes. She used the 'B' setting on her camera just to address the problem of the lack of light. Then she put the camera aside and took out her personal digital camera - her Sony 15 megapixel. This camera was able to give an excellent picture with a lack of noise that could be printed on a large poster of 10 metres without a loss in sharpness, clarity, or quality. For Mariam this wasn't enough, so she also recorded a two-minute video in which she included the stone and the site with all of the details of the inscriptions. Mariam felt so satisfied while she was putting her camera away that she found herself panting. At that point she realized that the ventilation in the hole was poor and the temperature was much hotter than it was outside. She needed to take off her heavy hooded rain jacket. But reasoning that the rain jacket was already stained from the descent, she decided to keep it on in anticipation of a difficult ascent. Recognizing the sound of Isaak's voice, she awoke from her thoughts to angry calls coming from above. He was furious, and she heard other voices yelling at him. She heard the deep voice of someone calling her name in an insulting tone and ordering her to get out right away. Though she didn't know what was happening up there, she felt her nerves preparing for a big fight. It was obvious that the coming moments would be very harsh and cruel.

Mariam climbed the wooden supports up towards the opening of the hole and when she peered up she found the young lieutenant standing above her. He extended his hand, but she ignored it, instead lifting herself out of the hole to stand up on her feet. She looked at his hand still stretched out, waiting; it turned out that he hadn't wanted to help after all.

"Give me the film that you shot. There are no pictures to be taken here and you must leave now."

As Mariam looked at Isaak, she found him surrounded by many people in civilian clothes and the signs of anger on his face. She heard him talking on his cell phone. It was obvious that he was trying to talk to an officer of high rank. Isaak's work had forged him connections with many high ranking officials in the police quarter and they were his prime sources that he usually dealt with on a daily basis. But it was obvious that 'the code' of journalists dealing with police officers was not going well at this moment. Mariam didn't hear very much of the conversation, but she heard him complying and repeating "Yes sir."

"The film please?" repeated the young lieutenant, stretching his hand out.

"How dare you," said Mariam in a violent tone, catching the officer off guard as she hit his hand away from hers. She continued in English. "Don't you ever touch me!"

The young lieutenant felt hurt and surprised by this unexpected violent attitude. He stretched out his hand, challenging her again, and grabbed her by the arm. She pushed him.

"Your arm deserves to be cut off. Respect yourself, otherwise I will roll you through the mud."

Isaak pushed through the crowd and stood in front of the lieutenant in support of Mariam.

"It is not your right to deal with journalists like this."

"If journalists don't know how to behave, we teach them the hard way."

"Okay, Pasha, we know how to get our rights back," responded Isaak threateningly.

He knew that tense conversations between policemen and journalists, when they happened this way, always ended in a friendly manner later on when a high ranking officer called the journalist with a very vague apology. The journalist would find himself obliged to accept this apology as he knew that the legal means of objections through the syndicate had to go through the maze of red tape which wasted the rights of the journalist in the end. It was very important to the journalist in these tense moments to protect himself so that he would never get physically hurt, as he was usually surrounded by many people who were working with the police including secret policemen. For any one of them it would be very easy, by a secret sign given by the officer, to start beating and hurting the journalist. At this time it would be hard to claim police brutality, as the policemen would rather claim that the unknown person had hurt the journalist. That was why Isaak had decided to go with what was called the 'withdrawing with threat strategy' which was also a very well known part of the secret code of dealings between cops and journalists.

"The most important thing now is to give me the film in the camera. No photos allowed," said the young lieutenant, trying desperately to finish the issue.

"Never in your wildest dreams," interrupted Mariam in a challenging voice, carefully avoiding the scolding look that had appeared on Isaak's face. She put her hand in her bag to bring out her journalist ID, saying, "I won't tell you I am a journalist because it wouldn't stop you." She produced another document from her bag and pushed it in the face of the lieutenant, adding in English, "But I am an American citizen who is threatening you for dealing with me like this. I would like to report you now and I will be requesting members of the American embassy to attend the investigation of this report."

With two fire-spitting eyes the young lieutenant looked at the American passport. He whispered in angry but understandable words, cursing America and its embassy, and he walked toward the car. He raised his voice, ordering his men to arrest Mariam and threatening that the American embassy would not be able to get her out of his hands.

He was confused, as he was just a low ranking officer. He didn't have enough experience to face such situations. When he went to the car he picked up the walkie-talkie and repeated this message. Then he made some calls on his cell phone while the thunder of the storm could be heard just above his head. The lighting struck twice and the rain started falling densely on the heads of everyone. Isaak looked at Mariam with much frustration and blame.

"What have you done? We don't want this to get bigger from nothing. You know very well that the whole story wouldn't deserve more than a small blurb on a tiny column on the front page."

Mariam smiled with confidence while tightening the hood of her raincoat and she said, "Sure. Because you weren't in the hole, you wouldn't mind giving up the film without fighting."

She was talking while her hand was in her camera bag, and a faint buzzing could be heard from within.

She continued, "Anyways, you seem to be right. I am ready to end this situation. Go ahead and do your magic to end this story before it gets bigger. We don't want to get more wet than this."

She said the last sentence with a certain sarcasm which Isaak did not appreciate. He looked at her suspiciously and then he held his cell phone to his ear. He tried to call his high ranking police officer in the quarter and then he headed towards the young lieutenant who was hiding in his car from the rain. They had a very short conversation, a part of which was intervened by the contact on Isaak's cell phone.

The negotiations didn't take long between Isaak and the young lieutenant. It was obvious that escalation wouldn't help any of the involved parties and so shortly thereafter Mariam had joined them in the police car. They then engaged in a conversation that contained more blame than anger. The young lieutenant apologized, claiming that he had 'just been following orders'. In turn, Mariam apologized, claiming that she had misunderstood what had been happening because she had been working in very difficult circumstances deep in the hole. The young lieutenant showed his appreciation for her courage in going down into the hole, and Mariam responded by complimenting the great effort the young lieutenant had shown in his work by staying late in the cold and the rain and being so accommodating on the scene. The exchange of the compliments opened the way for ending the confrontation, and when the moment came Mariam opened the camera, took out the film, and placed it in the hand of the young lieutenant who gave his word that he would keep an eye on it. He stated that the journal would be able to retrieve the film as soon as an official requisition would be made to the public relations department of internal affairs. Yet everybody knew that this would never happen.

A few moments later Mariam and Isaak were back in the journalists' car. The rains were once again hitting the windshield violently while the car travelled through the rainwater on the street towards the journal's building. And even though Isaak could not see his colleague because of the darkness of the night, he could hear her laughing in victory as she took out a small roll of film and put it in a small container.

"It's obvious that today's news is going to be published with photographs," laughed Isaak, hinting that he understood the game she had played. Mariam had taken advantage of the moment of confusion when she had shown her passport to the young lieutenant while quickly reloading the camera with a blank roll.

"I don't know what changed in the young lieutenant's mind to start treating us so poorly; it must have been the Curse of the Pharaohs," Isaak continued. Inspired by the sound and light, Isaak changed his voice to a more serious tone and began acting theatrically: "Beware of the Curse of the Pharaohs, for the curse will catch whoever wakes the sleeping pharaoh."

Although he was joking, Marian felt a mysterious trembling in her body. She didn't know why. Was this the Curse of the Pharaohs? Or perhaps her shaking was merely caused by her wet clothes on this cold night.

\*\*\*\*\*\*\*\*\*\*

DISCOVERY OF ARTEFACT AT THE SITE OF A DIGGING SEWAGE SYSTEM IN AINCHAMPS

<u>Written by Isaak Shoaib</u>

<u>Photographed by Mariam Gatas</u>

9th December

*The workers of the company Almocolum have discovered an artefact made of pink granite during the process of digging to extend sewage pipes into the district of Ain Shams. General Ahmad Hassan, the Ministry of Internal Affairs and the Head of the Cairo Police Quarter, received a report from the site manager regarding the discovery of an artefact bearing Pharaonic inscriptions while digging on Occasha Street, Ain Shams. In response to the unusual report, Colonel Mahmud Hosam, Head of the Police Quarter in Ain Shams and Major Saleh Sami, Head of Criminal Investigation with his two sergeants Ibrahim Ramadan and Solaiman Gafaar, arrived immediately on site. It was discovered that the artefact lay approximately seven metres under the earth. In light of this ancient finding, all work has stopped on the sewage system until the formation of a committee from the Ministry of Culture and the High Supreme Council of Antiquity to study the site of the artefact and decide upon its significance. General Hosain Ali, Manager of the National Project of Sewage, has declared that the recent discovery will not delay the work of the project as there are teams from the state working on improving the infrastructure of the capital city and extending the services to the poor and outskirt districts of the capital as part of the general plan of the Egyptian government to improve the standard of living of the average Egyptian and thereby relieve their suffering.*

Isaak reread the notes he had written on scrap paper and smiled at the last part that he had added as a compliment to the head of the sewage project who had a strong connection with the head of the journal. Even though the head of sewage had not been present at the site (he had probably been in bed sleeping at the time), Isaak had surrounded his name with flattering words so as to increase the possibility of garnering a rewarding effect later.

Isaak checked the article again for spelling and grammatical mistakes. He then headed to the chief editor's desk to admit the article before asking the secretary of publishing to put this news in the third edition of the journal. When the secretary of publishing asked him about the photos, Isaak called an internal number. He listened to the ringing for a moment before Mariam responded saying "Ten minutes until the developing is complete. The pictures are pretty good and you could publish two pictures with the news: one for the whole site and the other for the artefact. You will need at least four columns for the pictures to be nicely framed."

This amount of space would mean withdrawing practically two or three articles from the front page or possibly making them smaller and placing them on an internal page. It was the responsibility of the chief editor and the secretary of publishing to complete this mission while Isaak rushed to the photography department to see the pictures and to choose from among them which would be fit for the report.

Some people have an amazing ability to present themselves to others in a totally different way from who they are inside, and Mariam looked like a strong, stubborn, open-minded woman who had a good sense of humour with her colleagues. Yet when she was alone in her apartment all of her features changed dramatically. The smile and brilliance seemed to vanish from her face and be replaced by an expression of sad pessimism. Sometimes she didn't even care to turn on the lights and would just use the faint light coming in through the windows to light her way as she moved through her apartment. At times she moved as if she was escaping from the confrontation of the photos that hung on her walls. There were pictures of her husband Ismail, who she believed had been murdered two years prior (although the official reports said it was suicide), and pictures of her two kids Adam and Sarah, the most valuable things left for her in this world. She had been forced to give them up to live with their grandmother, the mother of Ismail, to avoid getting into a legal fight about custody and to be able to maintain a tolerable relationship with her husband's family after she had destroyed her relationship with her own family due to the marriage that she had never ever regretted.

Ten years ago, when she was in her fourth year of medical school, her heart had danced with joy when Ismail Mohamed Alkhazindar had confessed his love. Their relationship had developed along their student years from colleagues to friends to intimate friends despite the fact that he was her senior of two years. His older years had made him graduate before her and land a job as a teaching assistant at the university. Flooded with activity, enthusiasm, and intelligence, he was bighearted and had a wonderful personality. He belonged to a family some of whom had attained the title of Pasha during the royal period. Their relationship had violated the red lines, social regulations, and known rules and traditions of their respective religions. For her part, Mariam belonged to a Christian family from south Egypt. Her family was well known, wealthy, conservative, and powerful. Her father was a famous surgeon. Although he had lived for many years in America where Mariam had been brought up, his upper-Egyptian personality that he had always maintained made him strict and he refused to allow Mariam to marry a Muslim classmate.

"I would cut you in small pieces and toss you to the dogs."

Because her father had spent almost three-quarters of his life in the United States, it was hard for him to make a complete sentence in Arabic without using a few words from the English language. However, while at the peak of his rage his pure south Egyptian dialect would return in a fury. The words came out of his mouth as if they were bullets coming out of a gun machine.

Though her dad was angry, he would never go to the extent of doing what he had threatened to do. Instead, he decided to cut off all ties with her and act as though he had never had a daughter. The rest of her family's reaction was even harsher than her dad's. She could imagine her cousin ending this discussion by hitting her. Her Christian colleagues and friends dealt with her in a discarding and degrading way also.

Although her Muslim colleagues and friends had been, in the beginning, enthusiastic about her decision and had attended the couple's marriage ceremony, their relations had quickly became less warm. It seemed that they had hoped that her marriage to Ismail would be an introduction to converting her into a Muslim, but when months and years passed without Mariam changing her religion, their treatment and dealings with her had changed drastically and had grown colder and colder. She had faced a similar situation with Ismail's family. She remembered her first meeting with her mother-in-law when she had been presented with a small pamphlet bearing the title "Veiling before it's too late". She had gratefully accepted the gift, hiding her reservations and shyness. After that, from time to time she had received some female hints from her mother-in-law about the way she dressed, even though Mariam always, even in America, would dress modestly because this was the line which had been drawn by her father who had brought her up according to the Oriental Egyptian morals and traditions. She had also received hints from Ismail's family members about the privilege of Islam. They would pray for her so that God would light her path to the right religion, which in their minds was Islam. Strangely, the only person who never talked to her about this issue was Ismail himself. Although he was a devout Muslim who prayed regularly, fasted, and read the Qur'an, he never asked her to convert. To her this was a mystery she could never understand.

"Do you really believe, like your family, that my destiny on the Day of Judgment will be the flames of hell because I didn't convert?"

She had asked him this question once on a night when her eyes were tearstained after they had gathered with his family members on Ramadan eve. They had talked during this evening about paradise and hell and its hardships for the non-believers. These main lines were so similar in the two religions of Islam and Christianity with the followers of these religions adopting the same belief that the followers of the other religion would certainly be fated for hell. Their good deeds and graces didn't matter. Smiling at her in empathy, Ismail held a small Qur'an in front of her, opened it to a page, and asked her to read:

"No matter who believes, whether Christian, Jew or anyone else, it is the deeds that count."

He had whispered to her in a warm voice, "Don't worry too much about what people say; I would prefer a thousand times that you keep your own religion rather than change it to satisfy anyone else, even if that person was me. The most important thing is to keep a good relationship between you and your God full of belief and respect. Worship him because you believe he is mighty and wise and worth being worshipped, and do not be hypocritical to anybody or any society."

"Ohh, I lost the whole world and I won Ismail, which is a good deal, and I will never regret it," said Mariam to herself as she remembered the best days of her life.

*:*:*:*:*:*:*:*:*

There were many reasons why Mr. Mansi was the most hated journalist in the institution. These may have been the same reasons that had landed him his job as the chief editor. In the big governmental newspapers, the popularity of the chief editor among his colleagues and workmates was the least important qualification that the decision makers thought about when it came to making a decision about who got to sit in "the chair". The extreme love from Mr. Mansi to both the powers that be and the chair had resulted in the title Mr. Chair, the nickname that everyone in the institution used when they tried to talk secretly about him. They always made jokes about his loyalty to the decision makers, as they all knew that he had arrived at his highly ranked position thanks to his secret reports that he had been writing for over 40 years to the high security institutions about small or big occurrences that took place at the journal in its various ages.

These secret reports of Mansi had caused a lot of journalists and thinkers to end up in jail. The position of the head of publishing was a special prize from the high security institutions for their 'own men'. After all these long years of infamous reports, his chair had now become a barrier to his contact with the journalists and his reports had come to a stop.

His relationship with the secret service had become less intimate and was substituted by a big network of powerful businessmen and key players in the ruling party. Through this network he was trying to pave the way to a big jump, and maybe the last jump before his retirement. "Mr. Chair", the head of the institution and the most highly ranked in the national media, was sitting in the same chair that the intellectual giants of journalism, politics, and modern history had once sat upon. Now he was merely one step away from the biggest chair of all in the Egyptian governmental press. The most important thing was to enforce his golden rule of "Never say no to whomever has power."

When his mobile rang at six a.m. Mr. Mansi shook away his sleep right away. His nervous system after long years of work had adapted to light sporadic sleep and he had trained himself to wake up completely in just a few seconds when his mobile rang, especially when it was this number that not very many people knew - only those to whom Mansi's golden rule applied.

The phone call didn't take more than two minutes. After the call ended Mansi grabbed his other cell phone, the one he used for his everyday dealings, and made a phone call to the person who was responsible for staying overnight at the journal to ask him about the recent changes in the journal's third edition.

**********

In a Middle Eastern capital city, Jakov Panchiev took out his luxurious Cuban cigar box that he always kept in a safe. He was whistling a joyful melody to himself while preparing his suitcase for an urgent work trip he had been asked to carry out only a few seconds ago.

"You will go back to Cairo. Enjoy your time there," he advised himself.

He placed his cigar box in the suitcase carefully. The last time he had lit a cigar in Cairo was three months ago (last August) in celebration of accomplishing his latest mission there. His doctor would go crazy if he had known that Jakov was still smoking cigars from time to time. As an asthma patient his lungs couldn't bear being in the same room with a smoker let alone become accustomed to himself smoking. Yet he could not resist the temptation of the habit that had become a ritual in accomplishment of his special art.

"The one who deals with this job as merely a means of earning a living never goes far. You can make more money from smuggling caviar. The one who is in it for the thrills or excitement never goes far either. You can enjoy the same adrenaline from sky diving or skiing in the mountains of Aral. Real success comes to the one who deals with this job by considering it as a pure art, whose senses melt as the work bears one's own unique fingerprint. If you do not enjoy your job, then you will most definitely fail."

He remembered these words that he had been told by his ex trainer, Colonel Igor, the one who had been aptly named the Wolf of Sahoj. Colonel Igor was the leader of the team the Soft Angels - the most expensive, secret, and highly trained team in the KGB. This team was responsible for snuffing out those who the Kremlin deemed a potential danger or a harassment to the state of workers and farmers.

"Killing is easy but taking souls is an art."

So he had been told in the Soft Angels. "Any thief or criminal or even a ferocious animal could spill blood and leave a mess behind, but only the Angels would take souls without leaving any trace." These were the words of the Wolf making fun of religious mythology while teaching them how to deal with the crime scene. He taught them how to hide the traces of violence and torture that might be practiced with the victims if the objective was to obtain specific information before accomplishing the mission. The dead could not talk, but cadavers could speak volumes about the identity of the killer. That is why the Soft Angels had to perfect the art of silencing the cadavers whenever he wanted it to appear like a natural death. One must also perfect making the cadavers tell lies whenever they wanted it to look like a murder while leading the suspicion towards other parties.

Unfortunately the skills of Jakov were not appreciated enough in his homeland as the Big Bear had collapsed in 1991 and the KGB had disbanded after the failed attempt on behalf of Vladimir Kryczkov of murdering the last Soviet President, *Mikhail Gorbachev*. He was arrested and substituted by General Vadim Bakidim who had come for a specific mission which was disbanding the Soviet intelligence (KGB). This mission was officially accomplished on the sixth of November, 1991.

With the disbanding of the KGB, the Soft Angels had found themselves facing cold treatment from the new leadership. The open budget of the team had shrunk and the whole team was reformed. Tens of field agents had retired. The Wolf had lost his job and he had pursued his art with the Mafia instead. Jokov took an insulting hit to his dignity when he received a discharge notice deeming him 'medically unfit'. The supreme military committee considered his asthma a barrier in his service to the army. Jakov tore apart the paper, sacrificing any sort of worthless monthly compensation.

"I don't need your rubles. They are not worth the paper they are printed on. Damn them and damn you."

He shouted like this at the members of the committee facing a military trial for the charge of insubordination to his superiors. The Wolf of Sahoj had interfered to save his student from jail. Because of his new position working for the Mafia, he had lots of connections - even more than before. But when he offered Jakov the opportunity to work for him by serving money princess in Russia, Jakov had refused instantly - not because of any moral objections, but because to stay in the collapsing empire had become unthinkable.

"There are many in this world who will appreciate my art."

Jakov finished packing his suitcase and left to catch the first flight heading to Cairo.

*•*•*•*•*•*

Some nights are like a sack with holes which sleep fails to patch and where everything spills out the bottom. Memory can no longer persevere. Mariam rolled over in her bed listening to the moan of memories. Her gaze was locked in the space between her eyes and the eyes of Ismail, a gaze that stretched across three continents.

She had left for Baghdad, leaving Ismail behind in London and her kids with Grandma in Cairo. They would be spending their summer vacation there until Mariam was done with her urgent mission. It wasn't the first time she had taken part in covering wars. She wore her bulletproof vest on which the word 'Press' was written in big white letters, silently begging an anonymous sniper whom she would never know. In Baghdad the situation was different, where the white word was sometimes a magnet for bullets and rubble as if it was a Bull's-eye. Ismail welcomed these trips. "Truth needs to be told. Truth needs someone to tell it to the whole world," he would say. But she found that truth in Baghdad did not need journalists to tell it. Death was the only absolute truth. The Angel of Death was working days and nights filling the graves with bodies whose eyes had a permanent expression of surprise.

It was surprise in the eyes of the dead and fear in the eyes of the living. That's how the looks in Baghdad were divided.

"Why?"

The dead eyes shouted an everlasting question to which no one knew the answer.

The cadavers varied in colour, religion, race, sex, and wounds. Some wore American military suits and others wore typical Arab dresses or masks and donned kamikaze belts, but they are all alike in the colour of blood and in their gaze of surprise. Death looked at districts and streets. It stared in their eyes every morning, gritting his black smile and sharing with them their morning coffee, playing with them and with millions of other people who did not know the game of Russian roulette in the Iraqi style. The wheel spun and the pointer stopped on a set of eyes that would fill with surprise. Sometimes it would stop and there would be a look of fear, and then it would grit its teeth saying, "It's not your turn yet."

The Baghdadian death accompanied Mariam. Though it taunted and made fun of her, it never took her soul that was standing on its tip toes wearing the bull's eye. Instead, death went away to take her soul mate that was waiting in London and then whispered these words in a phone call across a great distance: "Ismail is dead. Ismail committed suicide. Ismail jumped from his balcony." He had left a message on his laptop apologizing for his sudden departure from life.

She had jumped across continents. In the cold morgue, Ismail had turned into a number and a preserved figure in a metal drawer. She had looked into his cold eyes which burned hers with tears. The British investigator who had accompanied her had given his condolences. She refused the idea that Ismail had committed suicide.

"Ismail is Muslim and Muslims never commit suicide."

The investigator pursed his lips, giving condolences which lacked sympathy. "You came from Iraq, didn't you? Muslims there commit suicide every day to go to paradise and marry their 70 virgins."

The investigator didn't understand that believers never committed suicide. Ismail could never have committed suicide. Rather, a crime had been committed and she knew the murderer. She had never imagined that her father would have one day executed his threat to take her soul mate in London while leaving her body in Baghdad soulless.

She remembered Ismail's words about her father. When the conversation at the end of a night met with the topic of her dad, Ismail would smile kindly. "I understand your dad, darling. Imagine if our daughter Sarah would marry without my acceptance. I would certainly be angry. The problem isn't that you married a man from a different religion. Your father is a scientist and science hinders religious fanatics. That isn't the core of the problem. The real problem is that you are a daughter who married against the will of her father. Your dad never lived in that moment of joy from shaking hands with the man who would share his life with you. He never looked in his eyes anxiously, searching for his daughter's future life. Any man who leads his life looking after his own young flower and keeping her away from hands and looks will in a moment find his young, dear flower opened with her scent attracting some stranger. I totally understand his feeling and expect that this crisis will part like a summer cloud."

"It was never a summer cloud, Ismail. It became a winter's storm that caused lightning and rained blood... your blood... and you were left with that look on your face staring in surprise at your murder."

*-*-*-*-*-*-*-*-*

The afternoon publishing meeting at the "Sphinx" usually started at one p.m. but Mr. Mansi always came to the building an hour or two early as he typically had appointments and interviews in the morning programs to defend the policies and decisions of the Egyptian government in the famous program *Good Morning Egypt*. His expensive Mercedes, which he had received care of the institution, arrived at the main gate of the building along with a four by four car dedicated to the bodyguards. When he entered through the main gate, two bodyguards accompanied him in civilian clothes. Always on the left side near the hip a big bulge under their coats concealed their weapons. This loud convoy was one of the reasons for the increasing hatred of the journalists. It had never happened before in the history of the institution that such extreme security procedures had been necessary for any of the leaders. Some of them had needed to be protected more than Mansi, but they hadn't ask for protection. They had experienced major threats because of their intellectual opposition to extremists who adopted violence and practiced assassination, but they had all simply walked the corridors in silence and dealt with the journalists and even the cleaning people with modesty and respect according to well known tradition. All the workers felt distaste when they saw this convoy penetrating the building as Mansi walked with his armed guards up to the editing hall. Even the holiest part of the journal, which represented the heart of this entity, was not safe from the raids of Mansi and his armed guards. However, after a few days of being the head of editing, he had given the convoy. He had been given a heavy warning from the higher powers that this kind of behaviour was provoking the journalists and could potentially lead to some kind of uncontrollable uprising. Forced to adhere to the orders, from that point on he had ordered his body guards to wait outside for him in the visiting room.

On that morning, Mansi's convoy had arrived earlier than usual. Before the clock struck eight a.m. the members of the night shift, who were getting ready to go home, had seen the convoy coming through the gates. Mansi's expression was stern. He was a stout man with his hair dyed black and his tired eyes announcing that he had not slept the previous night. When he sat down at his desk he took a quick look at the journal and made sure that his instructions were fulfilled. He turned on his computer and punched in his secret password that opened up all the locked doors. He logged in to his secret protected files and started searching the employee database looking for something. After a while he made a long distance phone call. When this ended he asked for Mr. Zakaria, the head of the photography department.

"In a few hours a very important guest will arrive and I have to be completely ready to cooperate with him," he said to himself smiling, remembering his golden rule: "Never say no to whomever has power."

*\*\*\*\*\*\*\*\*\**

On the phone she heard the laughing voice of Isaak on the other end.

"Good morning, Mariam. What a loss that the whole adventure evaporated in the air."

She didn't understand what he meant. Her ritual of waking up had not yet begun and the adventure of last night had made her leave the building of the journal before the release of the third edition to change her wet clothes that had been soaked by the heavy rain during the shooting of the artefact discovery.

"Good morning, Isaak. What do you really mean?"

"Haven't you read the third edition yet? The story came out very brief and without photos. Mr. Mansi called the desk responsible on night shift and ordered him to remove your photos."

"God damn this bastard," she found herself cursing in English before realizing that her colleague was still on the other line. She heard him laughing, and she yelled violently at him. "I haven't even woken up yet and you are laughing like this. Are you provoking me to go over there and give shit to that fucking bastard Mansi?"

He knew well that she meant what she said. Despite the cloud of arrogance that Mansi had around himself and although he often dealt with many in an abrupt, snobby way, he always tried to avoid those who might deal with him without fear and those who knew their personal and legal rights. He avoided those who would never let anybody violate their own red lines. And maybe he was paying a great deal of respect to Mariam in particular because of her famous family and her strict American way of behaving however she wanted. She always stuck to the official lines in her work relations. Her colleagues remembered well what had happened on her first day when Mr. Mansi had received her in his office along with the head of the photo department and two other freshly graduated photographers. He had welcomed them and said some well-structured sentences about the rules of work in the institution. He had pointed to her new colleagues and said to Mr. Zakaria in the usual cheap way he talked to those who worked for him:

"You have to deal with these kids strictly, Zakaria. There is no need to spoil them from the very beginning. I know you are too sissy."

Her face had turned red while seeing her weak boss shrinking and accepting the insult. He had whispered stupidly: "uh-huh."

She was completely surprised when she saw Mansi pointing at her and saying: "And here we've got a nice new American piece. This is the first time in the photo department that a skirt got in."

And then he winked, saying, "The photo department needs a nice breeze."

Mr. Zakaria had laughed shyly along with the two new photographers. She had responded sharply in English: "Excuse me!!?"

The sound of laughing melted before the fire coming out of her eyes while she continued in the same firm tone: "You have to watch your language!"

At this moment the face of Mansi had turned pale while he forced a fake laugh. Zakaria had tried to break the tension of the situation by making a few jokes. However, it was too late: the arrow had hit the target. All of the colleagues had known well from the way Mansi had dealt with her from then on that The American Girl Scout had earned her respect from everyone, even Mansi himself.

Isaak recalled this occasion of listening to Mariam on the other end vowing her revenge on Mr. Chair.

As much as he would have liked to see Mansi insulted in a heated conversation with this stubborn, south-Egyptian American girl, he was also afraid that his name would be mentioned in the issue. He responded by saying, "Let it go Mariam; this is not that important. There is a very strange issue in the news that made Mr. Mansi withdraw the photo file and the negative and the pictures related to it. He demanded that Zakaria bring him everything we had. But strangely, it had been totally withdrawn from the archive."

For the second time the blood rushed to Mariam's head and she blew up, saying, "Who the hell does this man think he is? It's not his right at all to do this. This is my own personal effort. The whole file and negatives are the property of the institution, and not his own personal belongings."

"For God's sake, Mariam," interrupted Isaak, laughing. "He is the big boss and it is his own right to do many things. We are in Egypt, not in America. No one has any rights except the boss. Try to live here in Egypt and remember that the big boss decides everything." He stopped laughing and began speaking in a serious way. "The most important thing that I have managed to do is save one single picture that had accompanied the news report. I hid it from Mansi's guillotine. And I know well that you shot another collection of pictures with your digital camera. Could you please give me some of them? I would love to make a real report with pictures for the independent journal. I think they would appreciate such a report and could even pay us good money. Let us at least get out of this shit on top."

Mariam could not help herself from smiling as she listened to his words. These were words that all young journalists used (and some experienced ones as well) when it came to talking about an extra source of income from the job. As most of the journalists in the government institutions were very low paid, many of them tried to find little extras on the side to make a decent living. One of the most famous ways was to sell their own reports and interviews to the independent competitive journals that were very gradually starting to take a bigger share from the governmental journals. Although it may have looked unfair to the institutions as its own personnel abused its potential and resources for the benefit of the competitors, this ideal, professional ethical criteria was not recognized in the world of failed governmental institutions which were led by people like Mr. Mansi (with his own stupid Golden Rule). And after all, the governmental journals had become pointless booklets that none of the readers trusted. These journals didn't care about anything except satisfying the rulers and the people with power in their hands.

"Well Isaak, I will publish some pictures for you and you will need to complete the report by consulting some real archaeologists and experts, not those fake declarations that you got from the Head of the National Project of City Sewage saying that the artefact has no monumental value and that it's just a prototype copy of artefacts filling the stores or Egyptian museums." [1]

Mariam ended the conversation and her brain totally woke up. She stretched her arms, jumped from her warm bed, and immediately started her morning exercises. She practiced some martial arts which followed the school of Shi Do Ki Kan.[2] After taking a cold shower while singing a nice song, she listened to the kettle whistling and then prepared a heavy breakfast. Next she sat at her laptop downloading some of

---

[1] There are almost 120,000 artefacts which are not currently exhibited and which are simply piled inside the darkness of the storerooms of the Egyptian Museum in Cairo.

[2] One of the full contact styles of karate famous in America, Japan, and Europe.

the pictures from the digital camera. "It is very strange what Mansi has done. What the hell made him withdraw the pictures from the article?" she wondered.

She opened up the window to let the dull winter sun rays enter after the rainy night but the sky was cloudy, warning of more rains to come. She went out to her balcony to wash her face in the cold sun's rays. From a side angle of her balcony, she gazed at the Nile River flowing quietly amongst the loud car horns and the crowds of people in Cairo. She remembered many years before that the scene of the Nile from her window had been much clearer. She remembered the warm nights she had spent with Ismail here. This is where she had made her decision.

"I don't want to continue my medical studies. I can't see myself in this career any longer. I want to be liberated from this choice that was dictated by my father as his wish."

Ismail smiled kindly. He had realized that she just loved her photography and wished to study it, and so he had a small surprise for her. He had already applied for her to study photojournalism in London. She would be with him while he did his Masters, as he had recently been awarded a scholarship from the University of Oxford. Hearing Ismail's idea she had been filled with happiness and had given him a big, warm hug. He had kissed her on her lips and then she had melted in his hands. In front of them the moonlight was reflected on the Nile's water.

It was very unfortunate that even the view of the Nile had changed upon her return to Egypt. She had found a recently constructed skyscraper full of condos, and this had become a barrier between her balcony and the view of the Nile. There was nothing left between the space except for the width of the street which lay in front of her. On the other side of the street was the medical school of Cairo.

*\*\*\*\*\*\*\*\*\*\**

"Bad news," said Professor John Howard to himself in a loud voice. The weak light of his computer screen reflected on his face in the middle of the darkness in a satanic way. The recent hours had been gruelling with the famous Professor busy making continuous phone calls and sending emails around the world. He had activated a network of allies and followers who served the ancient protocol.

"Never let anything be a coincidence."

This was a basic rule in the protocol that had to be completely and strictly followed. The information that had come a few hours earlier had seemed to be more than mere coincidence as soon as it had been added to the database of his already complicated personal computer.

The computer screen alerted him with a red flash and a small window appeared bearing a picture of a young Middle Eastern man. On top of his picture a black sign bore the word 'Done'. Beside it was a date from two years ago. Under the picture was the man's full name: Ismail Mohamed Alkhazindar. The facial expression of Professor Howard grew serious while his fingers typed away on his Blackberry. He wrote a message composed of six words. He hesitated a little bit and gasped deeply while hitting the send button. The message read: "Now you can light up your cigar."

*\*\*\*\*\*\*\*\*\**

Building number 133, Al Manial Street, was known by everyone in Cairo as the doctor's building because of its close proximity to the Medical School. The most important doctors of the school and of Egypt had chosen this building to be the on-campus clinic. In that way they could easily transfer between the school hospital and their private clinics.

Fourteen years earlier the famous surgeon Dr. Yahia Gatas had given a precious gift to his daughter on the occasion of her being admitted to the school, as this had been his greatest wish. The present was his own clinic keys to an office in this building.

"From now on this clinic is yours. You will need to live close to the university during your studies, and after graduation it will be the best beginning for your career. I achieved all my fame and success thanks to this clinic, although I unfortunately had to close it in more recent years due to my work commitment in Boston."

At that moment the gift had made her so happy. She had recognized its intangible value to her father. She had agreed to apply for med school as her dad had wished, but despite her degree being from America he had refused to allow her to attend medical school there.

"But medical studies in America are way better, Dad."

"Egypt is your own homeland, honey, and you will never know your homeland in a real way unless you live in it and feel its own pains. Live the university life in Egypt with its sweetness and bitterness. Deal with the poor patients at the university hospital and then you will feel a huge positive energy of light and happiness while you participate in relieving their pains. Just try it for one year, and if you don't like it I promise I will let you register at the biggest American university."

She knew that dreamy, romantic side of her father when it came to talking about Egypt, but she also realized that what he was saying was only a half-truth. Her dad's Middle-Eastern conservatism was very sensitive to the American university way of life, which included the clubbing, the boyfriends, and the keg parties. "Their values are totally different than ours," he had always insisted on saying.

"The Southern Egyptian in America."

She used to joke with him in this way whenever he made comments about how she was dressed or her adolescent adventures that all of her classmates were living. Then he would laugh saying,

"What's wrong with Southern Egyptians? I am proud to be so. Our roots go back 7,000 years in history."

Although Mariam Gatas had cut off her relationship with her dad ten years ago, and although she had also cut off her relations with the med school and its practices, she had kept that old clinic where she had lived the happiest moments of her life after marrying Ismail. In every corner of the apartment and on every single stair there was a dear memory that she could not afford to forget. When she came back to settle down in Cairo, she had chosen to live in her old apartment even though the noise and the harassment were excessive for a space in a building full of clinics.

All of the medical specialties existed in this building with constant visitors to the clinics from early morning until late at night. That is why when a cab stopped in front of the building and released two men that crossed the entrance, the men did not catch any special attention. One was a dark-skinned young man in his thirties wearing jeans and holding an envelope on which the symbol of the journal SPHINX was inscribed, and the other was thin and tall with foreign European features. He looked like he was in his fifties, but had maintained an excellent physique. Between his fingers there was a luxurious Cuban cigar that had yet to be lit. You could tell that he was waiting for the chance to light it.

*********

Hannah Gabriel had a very strange feeling sitting at her personal computer in her office. She wore evening attire which was composed of a short skirt and a completely naked back. Her skin felt the touch of the leather chair every time she leaned back. She was also wearing nine centimetre heels in the style of DG. They had cost a fortune. A few moments ago she had been immersed in bright lights adorned by brilliant jewels, perfume scents, and official complimentary smiles, but a sudden text message on her mobile had caused her to immediately leave the HSA's annual party She had even left behind the President of the United States along with a group of the most important academics, politicians, and media people in the world to follow her boss who was doing something mysterious in his office. And in spite of the weak light in his office, she noticed right away that he was tired and close to collapsing.

"Have I missed something, or has the world been invaded by aliens?" she queried with a beautiful grin stretched across her lips.

He sighed, trying hard to return the smile.

"I wish so on the condition that me and you were the only two survivors and it was up to us to keep the species alive."

She responded, trying to be serious.

"Hmm... A sign that our night will be a long one, my dear."

And then she whispered to herself, cursing her bad luck, "The vice president was about to invite me to dance with him but I left that opportunity to hear the flattery of the weird old professor."

"Tonight I have a mission for my special hacker."

"But remember, I never like to wear the black hat, as my hat must always stay grey." [3]

When it came to computers and the internet, Hannah was one of the most brilliant minds in the field. The federal electronic security service had classified her as a grey hat. Her friends had given her the nickname 'Hacky Hannah', and her resume contained a degree from Cornell University and two years of graduate studies in the federal

---

[3] A black hat hacker violates computer security out of maliciousness or for personal gain, while a grey hat hacker may surf the Internet and hack into a computer system for the sole purpose of notifying the administrator that their system has a security defect.

security systems as an administrator of internet. Also included was a four-page report describing an instance when she had managed to hack into the main server of the CIA during a session of training in security systems. She had developed a model for firewalls that was recognized by the CIA to recover the weak points and get to the holiest of holies in the American computer system.

The mission she was expected to execute tonight seemed from the outside to lie in the grey area, although Hacky did not feel ethically comfortable in fulfilling it.

*************

"Your threats never scared me, Mariam. I am ready to fight for my money, and then I either kill or am killed."

Mariam's lips pouted in shock while reading the text message on her cell phone. The phone number indicated her colleague Isaak. For the first moment she thought it might have come to her by mistake and that it was meant for someone else, but when she re-read the message she found her name written clearly at the beginning of the message. In surprise she hit the button to call Isaak. The reply was an automated message:

"The customer you have dialled is unavailable."

She tried a few more times.

"That's really weird. Something must be up, or else this is a bad joke from a harassing friend." She dialled the number of the journal and recognized the voice that answered. It was Joseph, her colleague in the department of editorials. Joseph was the last person she wanted to speak to.

"Good afternoon, Joseph; it is me, Mariam. Mariam Gatas."

After a moment of silence, she heard him clearing his throat and answering her greeting with scattered words.

"Could you please tell me if Isaak is at the editing hall?"

Then came a moment of silence that seemed like he was scanning the place with his eyes. He answered:

"No Mariam. Isaak is not there. You can call him on his mobile."

"I tried but he is out of service. Thanks anyway."

Mariam quickly finished the call without waiting for a response. For the last nine months she had spent at the journal she had been trying desperately to avoid Joseph and he her. A thick fence of cold ice always adorned their morning greetings and the simple necessary words that they had to exchange due to the nature of their work relationship. In her first week at the journal she had found the name of Joseph Ali on a work order that she had to fulfill with him in the field. She had asked the head of the department to include Joseph thinking that he didn't know about her return to Egypt. She had imagined that her appearance would be a happy surprise for him, as only a few years prior they had rarely been separate from each other at work. Later she learned that he had cancelled the work order when he had found out that she was the photographer. Zakaria had not informed her directly of the reason, but she had heard some ironic hints from her colleagues.

Mariam shook her head, trying to shed this bad memory from her mind, and again she began to ponder the meaning of the text message. "There must be a mistake." She furrowed her brow and gritted her teeth. She whispered in a high voice to herself, "You will pay dearly for this silly mistake, Mr. Isaak."

*-*-*-*-*-*-*-*-*-*

Experts in hacking are always called computer rats as they are like vermin working in darkness, locked away in their virtual burrows. Normally, they are just shy, socially awkward people who eat fast food while dripping ketchup and soda pop on their clothes and spending most of their time between the keyboard and the screen. They rarely have a social life outside of Facebook or Myspace.

Hannah however, was totally different, at least in this past year. Hannah had been born 25 years ago with a defect in the valves of her heart. The doctors at that time had believed that for her to live to 10 years old would be a miracle. Because of that, she had spent most of her childhood in bed. She had never practiced sports, and she had never played like other children. By the age of 12, not only had she managed to still be alive, but she had managed to beat Natalie Karbov, the world champion in chess, through the internet which had been set up by a charity organization which supported those who had cardiovascular disease. The research centres had raised money to utilize her help in developing computers. When she was 15, she had participated in the developing of "Deep Blue". This was a chess program that had raised its level of artificial intelligence to the point where it could challenge world champions in chess.

At the age of 21 Hannah had experienced a rebirth because of a surgery which was the first of its kind. This surgery had essentially reconstructed her heart from scratch. Hannah became able to move, laugh, stay up all night, and live a normal life. She finally left the cocoon she had been forced to live in during her years of sickness. She no longer belonged to the world of typical computer rats who stayed in their virtual burrows. For the first time ever she had a real social life which included getting dressed up and enjoying parties. She had a list of priorities, the top of which was dancing with the vice-president of the United States, but she had never lost her skills in the computer world. The job Professor Howard had asked her to do was not so hard, probably average in difficulty. It wouldn't take a long time. After all, she was a professional hacker.

Hannah took off her expensive heels to feel more comfortable. She placed a couch cushion behind her to separate the skin of her warm naked back from the cold leather of the chair. She started hitting the keyboard to complete a small hacking task. Professor Howard had given her the email address of a woman living in Egypt. He had given her the IP number of the woman's computer as well. All she had to do was to get inside all of this woman's online accounts including social media and email and search for any uploaded pictures in the last 24 hours.

"Is the old professor being blackmailed by a woman living in Egypt? Has she shot him in embarrassing positions and is threatening to post them?" thought Hacky Hannah, smiling cunningly. She expected to be surprised by an image of the respectful professor naked and kneeling under the feet of a whore wearing a Pharaonic costume.

✿✿✿✿✿✿✿✿✿

Working in journalist institutions usually allowed for a flexible timetable, except for the necessity of attending the morning editing meeting at ten a.m. and the afternoon editing meeting at one p.m. Most journalists did not have a strict timetable for working in the building as their job required them to be outside for long hours meeting sources, conducting interviews, and completing field reports. But some other departments did not have the luxury of flexibility like the editing desk and the photography department. They worked according to a strict shift system that required most of them to be physically present by nine a.m. Despite this expectation Mariam was not considered late, even by a little, when she got to the building at three p.m. Since she had worked the night shift, she didn't have to be in until six p.m. That was why it was strange how Zakaria received her. He was nervous and anxious.

"Where have you been, Mariam? I was about to call you."

"What's wrong, Mr. Zakaria? As you know I was on the night shift and didn't get back until late last night."

"Never mind that. The chief of editing is asking for you."

"Mr. Mansi? Why?"

"I really don't know, but he insisted that you get to his office as soon as you arrive."

Mariam left the head editing office wearing an expression of deep thought. She appeared as though she had just left a hypnosis session.

"I just don't understand."

She held her Blackberry in her hand and tried to make sense of the last ten minutes. She tried to understand what that old fuck had meant while silently blaming herself for allowing him to control her when he was talking. It had paralyzed her. It had been such a surprise that Mansi would have asked to meet with her after all the situations she had shared with him and the way she had treated him during most of their meetings. This had made him avoid dealing with her directly. She had been happy about that, as Mansi was known for sexually assaulting other female workmates.

The chief editor had received her with a sickly, sticky smile. When she stretched her arm out to shake his hand, a chill ran through her as the palm of his hand had the feeling of a snake. The chief had pretended to look busy by talking on the phone. He asked his secretary that they not be disturbed and to not let anyone else in the room.

"What you did yesterday with that police officer was a big mistake. It is not a good idea to mess around with cops, don't you think?"

Mariam understood right away that he was talking about her trick last night of keeping some of her materials.

"Is that the reason why you withdrew the photo file from the photography department?"

"It is not the only reason. Listen Mariam, Isaak Shoaib asked to meet me today and he told me some things that I couldn't believe. It seems to me like you are in a lot of trouble."

Mariam had no idea what he was talking about. Did this have anything to do with the mysterious message from Isaak? She looked at Mansi questioningly and was about to respond, but he interrupted her. He emphasized every syllable of his speech and chose his words carefully:

"Listen Mariam, every one of us comes to a point in our lives when we have to make a decision. You are a smart, educated girl and you have a lot of personal and professional experience. A few powerful people have told me to pass along a message to you. Now, I don't know about the details and I don't want to know. This is the real wisdom, as it is wrong to challenge what you do not know."

He handed her a Blackberry.

"Take this - somebody will call you on it. I advise you to do whatever he says."

\*\*\*\*\*\*\*\*\*\*

The sound of a piano flowed through the computer's speakers and the voice of Elton John could be heard singing the words: "Your candle melted and the story is over. Too early for the end." This was the first thing any visitor would find when they entered the blog that bore the name "Candle in the Wind". This was Mariam's blog.

Like a professional thief, Hacky Hannah had gotten into the blog as if she was sneaking in on the tips of her toes. A few seconds earlier she had gotten into Mariam's personal email account and she had made sure that no pictures or hidden scheduled files had been uploaded during the last 24 hours. She also blocked the possibility of any files being uploaded on those pages as Howard had instructed. He asked her again to make sure that there were no pictures uploaded on her personal blog. From there she searched any other personal accounts that Mariam might have like YouTube or FileShare or any other account used for uploading files. For a professional like Hannah, this was easy. But some sad shadows marked her soul after she discovered something on Mariam's Facebook page that made her feel uncomfortable.

"Like a candle in the wind I have lived in my life. It isn't easy for anyone to listen to the heart among the noise. God made everyone have their own personality. It is not a coincidence that everyone has their own fingerprints and it is not a coincidence that everybody has their own DNA in every cell. God made us that way. He never wanted us to be prototypes. God's will is that every one of us keeps their right of being different and unique, even in our ways of worshipping him. Those claiming to speak in the name of God want people to be like a herd of penguins: drawing their lives in black and white, having wings and never flying, and being millions of heads and beaks scattered over the ice. They want all people to have the same features and behaviour, without anyone exerting the right to be different. If God had wanted he would have made us all the same, but he was so wise that he wanted us to be unique and different.

"That right of being different and unique I lived and practiced every single day of my lifetime. I grew up as an Egyptian in American schools and then as a girl in a society of men. When I traveled to cover the war in Iraq, everyone looked at me as the other who he denies; the opposite who he will not trust. Americans treated me with suspicion because I was Arabic, Muslims never trusted me because I was Christian, and Christians never accepted me because I was married to a Muslim. Everyone thought badly of me: a woman working in a man's profession. Nobody ever talked to me using the pronoun 'we'. Instead, they used the pronoun 'you', only they were they. Separate pronouns that never ever met in one sentence."

Hannah scrolled down the lines of the blog. There was nothing there to indicate that the old protocol had been violated.

*************

When the Blackberry rang in Mariam's hand the sound took her out of her daydreaming state which she had been in since exiting Mansi's office. On the other end she heard a voice speaking perfect Arabic in a Syrian way but with a foreigner accent that could be identified when he tried to pronounce certain sounds.

"Hello Mariam. You have something that doesn't belong to you, and I want you to hand it back to me."

"Who are you?"

"The pictures of the artefacts that you shot yesterday. You have to hand them to me. I advise you not to keep any electronic copies."

"Who are you?"

"I know that you are stubborn. All of them have told me so, but I have the cure of obstinacy. I will send you a nice gift that will make you a lot wiser when dealing with me."

The call ended as abruptly as it began. After a moment the Blackberry sounded a bleep to indicate that there was an unopened message.

When she opened the file she gasped loudly and her features contorted in fear.

*************

"Mariam, are you okay?"

Mariam awoke from her daze to the sound of Joseph's voice who had appeared in front of her. His eyes conveyed a worried look like she never seen before, at least not for a long time.

"What happened; did you see the devil?"

He didn't know how right he was in asking that question. Her hands were still holding the Blackberry and the signs of shock were still evident on her face. This prompted him to lead her to the visitors' room which was only a few steps away from where they were. He rushed to the water cooler and brought her a plastic cup of water. She accepted with shaking hands and thanked him, swallowing it all in one shot. She sighed, trying to hold herself together.

"Your whole body is shaking. Did that animal try to molest you?" he asked her firmly.

"Whom do you mean?"

"The old adolescent - the Chair. What did he do to you? I know that he asked you to see him right away and that he met you on his own. I know that he asked his secretary not to let anyone in his office. Then I saw you leaving, looking abnormal. I followed you while you were walking and..."

She hadn't seen Joseph when she had left the office of the chief editor, as she had not been in the right state to notice such things. Suddenly the meaning of Joseph's words dawned on her. She said, "How did you know all of this? Were you watching me? Why were you following me that way?"

Joseph felt embarrassed by the unexpected attack and he stuttered back, "It's normal that I care about you. You are part of the family in a way and I wouldn't want that asshole molesting you or hurting your reputation."

This was the first time in her life that she had heard Joseph describe her as a part of the family. There was really no genetic relationship between them, only by marriage, with Joseph being the cousin of her husband. There had once been an even stronger relationship than blood, which was their friendship that had suddenly gotten cold once she had married Ismail. The three of them had always been best friends. Long years ago Joseph, Ismail, and Mariam had rarely been apart. All of their classmates had made fun of Joseph when they saw him at the medical school every day. They were always joking with him saying that he should transfer his papers from the faculty of media to the medical school. He used to laugh, answering, "I wouldn't want to be a butcher or an undertaker," referring to the anatomy lectures that he would sit in on. The reality was that Joseph was attending the medical school more than he was attending his own media school. He spent all his time in the faculty garden and the student lounge. He didn't even attend his own university excursions because he was always with Ismail and Mariam and the other medical students.

"I got to med school on my own; I got in and it was my choice. After long, long years, I graduated as a butcher's apprentice."

Joseph used to sing that song in an attempt to provoke Mariam's classmates. He had written it himself for the class trips. It took them a long time to return with a comeback until Ismail wrote his own response using the same melody as Joseph's song:

"I got to media school on my own; I got in and it was my choice. After long, long years, I graduated as a newspaper stand owner."

Ismail used to sing this song by raising his voice on the last syllable, pointing with his arm and hand, imitating a newspaper salesman calling the crowds to buy his goods. The bus group would erupt in laughter. Then the accompanying drum rhythm would change and they would go into a scout song that everyone knew.

She felt the shadow of these memories, those sweet days. She smiled, and maybe the brilliance of that grin scattered Joseph's thoughts for a moment as well. Feeling shy, he turned his face away from her while trying to decode the meaning of that smile. He felt ashamed of himself, his face turning red, as she had busted him with the charge of watching her. He felt like negating the charge would make it stick to him even more.

"To tell you the truth, I was worried by the way Mansi was acting. This is the first time that he has asked to see you in his office, and he wanted to be with you alone there. And a friend of mine in the personnel department told me something weird."

She perked up, and looked at him questioningly.

He continued, "Mansi searched in the personnel database looking for your personal information, and when he didn't find your home address in your file, he asked his office manager to keep asking your department head and the institution's drivers for it until he got it."

At that moment the picture she had seen a few moments ago jumped back into her head. Very tense now, she asked Joseph frantically, "Why?"

"I have no idea."

"How did you know this? Are you following Mansi as well?" She found herself smiling slightly at the accusation.

He laughed and replied, "Uh no - A journalist never reveals his sources, but this is not the point. Mansi also asked for the personal data of Isaak the crime reporter. And then you called me today looking for him, and then I thought..."

She was shocked by the last sentence. She looked to her hand and found it wrapped tightly around the Blackberry with the horrible photograph still opened. In it, her colleague Isaak was sitting lifeless on her living room chair, his face covered in blood. His eyes were coldly staring into nothingness, void completely of the brilliance of life. In the background she saw the picture of her kids hanging on the wall. The living room of her apartment was a horrifying crime scene. Before she attempted to talk, the Blackberry alerted her once more with the same unknown number appearing on the display. She heard herself answering with a voice that seemed to come up from the depths of the earth.

She heard the whisper of a voice come through the Blackberry:

"Now I think you have become wiser and are more able to cooperate. Would you agree?"

"Is this some kind of sick joke? This picture can't be real."

"It is completely real, Mariam. You will now be accused of the crime of murder in the first degree. You killed Isaak. His body is in your apartment and the weapon bears your fingerprints. How will you explain to an inspector the existence of a cadaver in your apartment's living room?"

"You are crazy! You must be crazy!"

"Even the motive for the crime exists, as it seems that you stole some artefacts from the discovery site where you were yesterday. It seems that you dealt with Isaak so that you wouldn't have to split the earnings. It seems that you had a fight because you did not agree on what your share should be. So you came up with a plan to ask him to your apartment. Then you killed him."

Mariam's heart sank down to the floor. The letters of the weird text message she had received from Isaak appeared before her eyes once more.

"You are the one who sent the message! You-"

Her voice was similar to an old car engine struggling to start. But her mind was working at lightning speed, jumping from introductions to conclusions. She figured that the investigators would analyze the data on the victim's cell phone and they would indeed find the message that would for sure be used as evidence against her. Again she heard the hissing voice from the other end laughing and coughing and then saying,

"The artefact is already in your apartment. The chief editor will testify that Isaak had told him this morning that you both found the artefact and that you betrayed him and wanted to keep it for yourself. The chief editor has been very cooperative. He won't mind adding a small lie to his testimony in a way that would tighten the rope around your neck. I need you now to be completely cooperative, because in a few moments the cops might get a report about the crime. If they get into your apartment and find the body, then it will be too late to help you as the bullet will be in the air with no one to stop it. You will find yourself facing the gallows on your own. Therefore, I need you to be cooperative. I am the only one on earth who can save your pretty little neck on the condition that you do whatever I instruct you to do."

*************

Jakov Banshiev hung up the phone. His facial features were covered by a tight grimace, and rapidly he put the puffer inside his mouth and took a long and deep haul. He instantly felt better. Although he was hearing a deep whistling inside his chest, he took a breath and felt happy after the moment of thrill. He had lit his first cigar in two months. He felt that his lungs were rebelling against him from the recent phone call, but he had managed with an iron will to keep down his need to cough. He had played with the nerves of his victim in order to put her under his complete control. His victim was not supposed to hear any sort of weakness in his voice. If he had gotten into a fit of coughing, he would have broken the psychological wall that he had to keep between himself and his victim. In his training he had been taught how to make her completely receptive to his will.

Jakov took a deep breath saturated with another dose of Ventolin, and after his air passages were clear with oxygen he finally smiled. Everything had been carried out with ease, precision, and accuracy. It hadn't taken him long to convince the journalists that he was a foreign archaeologist working in Egypt who was interested in the pictures of the recently discovered artefact and that he would pay whatever amount was needed for them. He had seen greed in the eyes of the journalist while the man was talking about money, and so he had managed to trap him into accompanying him to the apartment of the photographer.

The journalist had walked to his death thinking that the apartment was the office of the foreign archaeologist.

Jakov looked at the fresh cadaver and moved away with care, making sure that his steps would not touch the pool of blood on the floor. He walked toward the wall and looked carefully at the picture of Mariam with her husband.

"A weird coincidence... because of a similar picture lots of plans in the past few hours have changed... as the old protocol says, 'never leave anything to coincidence.'"

The chief editor at the paper was extremely cooperative. Most importantly, he was never curious. Not in the least. On the contrary, he was keen not to know any details about the nature of the mission that Jakov was carrying out. He had given all the needed personal information about the journalist and the photographer, and that data had helped the leadership to make its decision.

"Now you can light your cigar."

Jakov looked at what was left of his lit cigar and he put it out. The remains were carefully sealed in a plastic bag which he would dispose of later. It was very important to keep the crime scene clean of any undesirable traces. Then from his pocket he brought out another cigar that was still in its tube.

"Very soon I will light my next cigar, but first I must wait for the order."

That is what Jakov thought to himself while his body buzzed from a charge of adrenaline. He imagined the upcoming thrill.

*\*\*\*\*\*\*\*\*\*\**

"So far it's negative. There is nothing showing that Mariam had uploaded any pictures on the internet in the past twenty-four hours."

"Great. When will you be able to give me the final result?"

"Give me some time. Less than two hours, probably. I need to make sure that she had no other account under any other names... but..."

Hacky Hannah hesitated slightly. She looked away from her boss who was drowning in an endless series of phone calls and emails. Cutting off her words that lay waiting on the tip of her tongue, she left the room. Her eyes were lit with a strange look. It was a mixture of sadness, confusion, and insistence.

*\*\*\*\*\*\*\*\*\*\**

Winter's dull sunset was setting quickly, as if it was being strangled by the clouds and dying suddenly without taking the time to cast its all too familiar orange glow on the horizon. The rains were dominating the streets and alleyways that appeared almost vacant, despite the fact that night had not yet come with its darkness.

When Mariam left the building and was faced with this weather, she felt like she needed this heavenly shower to be awakened and refreshed.

The past moments were wrapped in the dense fog that dwelled in her mind so that they seemed surreal. She couldn't realize what was happening when she had ended the phone call, as she had been fluctuating between consciousness and unconsciousness. She couldn't determine the true details of the situation. She did however recall very well the touch of Joseph's hands and his worried expression that was balanced between longing and care and other things. The fog surrounded her mind like a curtain while she told Joseph about the last series of strange events. She couldn't tell him all of the details, as she didn't know most of them herself. She didn't know why it had happened the way it had... was she crying?... Or had the tears froze in her eyes from the shock? The feelings and emotions had interfered and the thread of logic had vanished - the very logic that could have brought everything together in one ordered, rational line. All she knew was that she had come face to face with an unknown enemy. This was an enemy that wanted to enforce his own conditions and rules and that had the power to destroy her life. This enemy would put a rope around her neck. She stood at the front doors of the journal, breathing the cold air and bathing her soul with the cold mist while Joseph left to bring around his car that was parked some distance away. The horn of his car woke her up from her daze and she spotted him waving at her to get in. Her feet slipped into a pool of water while she was descending the front steps of the building. And then suddenly she was contained in the warmth of the car and surrounded by the soothing voice of Joseph who was explaining his plan.

"I've just made a phone call to a friend of mine who could help us understand what is happening. He is waiting for us now." He smiled despite the tense circumstances. "Unfortunately all we are missing in the coming mission is a hash cigarette."

*************

"Ratio est qua vitam."

A sentence written in Latin hung in the office of Dr. Yahia Gatas. To him it was the best explanation of his own philosophy on life. The literal translation of the sentence was "Discipline is what makes life." These words represented an incarnation of the philosophy of St. Paul, who used to consider God to be 'the God of Discipline'. Everyone who contemplated the universe would see a natural discipline and order and if one was to look at the human body, they would see a discipline incomparable to anything else.

"There are no clever surgeons or failed surgeons, but there are disciplined surgeons and chaotic surgeons. Chaos in the operating room means committing the crime of murder in the first degree."

That's how Dr. Gatas used to receive his students and his surgery colleagues who had been chosen based on long years of skill to accompany one of the most well known heart surgeons in the world as he practiced his magic in the operating room.

Because of his almost compulsive obsession with discipline and precision, all the workers in the hospital of the Sacred Heart in Boston used to call Dr. Yahia the 'God of Discipline'. For the past 20 years the sacred discipline had been breached only once three years ago when the White House had urgently called Dr. Yahia to perform a critical surgery in the heart of the American president. That was why it was a complete surprise for Dr. Solomon Isradowski, who was the second in command next to Dr. Yahia in the cardiology department of Sacred Heart, when he found out from Yahia's assistant that the good doctor had cancelled all of his appointments for that day. The assistant had delivered the message that Dr. Isradowski was to take over all of Dr. Yahia's appointments.

"Is Dr. Gatas okay? Is he suffering some sort of health problem?" asked Dr. Solomon.

"Dr. Gatas is fine, but he got a phone call a few moments ago and left his office abruptly. He asked me to cancel his appointments today."

"Was the phone call from the White House? Is the President changing his heart valve again and Dr. Gatas must intervene once again to save the world?" asked Dr. Solomon sarcastically.

"I have no idea, but I think it was an official phone call," the assistant answered in an extremely curt manner.

"It must be the Day of Judgement if the God of Discipline is messing around with his own philosophy," Dr. Solomon muttered to himself. He nodded his head to end the conversation.

*:*:*:*:*:*:*:*:*:*

A few years ago the academic pillars of Egypt had been shaken by a big scandal that had surrounded one man: Dr. Yonas Idris, who was one of the most famous Egyptologist at the University of Cairo. His CV included a PhD from Germany, and he was head supervisor of the UNESCO project in the Middle East and leader of many archaeological missions that had achieved groundbreaking discoveries. Because of all his credentials and achievements, the academic circles had nominated him for several international positions in the cultural field. Some had bet on him being a candidate for the Minister of Culture, and others had thought that his path was paved to be the head of the UNESCO organization. But this CV was torn to shreds one night during a routine police chick point. The doctor had been travelling at a late hour from a National UNESCO conference. The purpose of the conference was to assemble various political figures and other important people, including the general secretary of the United Nations, in hopes of petitioning for the protection of archaeological sites that were at risk due to current urban sprawl. Before the doctor had arrived at his house in the Almohandesin district, the police block had stopped him by coincidence for a routine check of driver's licence and verification of identity. No one knew exactly how the situation had escalated into a full-blown search of the car, but nonetheless the police had found a large amount of hash and other drugs. What made it even worse was that a blood analysis confirmed that the doctor had consumed drugs that evening. Rapidly the tabloids got a hold of the story and the headlines read, "Esteemed professor attends conference under the intoxication of drugs". One caricature artist had drawn up a cartoon of professor Yonas Idris in front of the great pyramids acting as a tour guide. The accompanying text read: "It took them twenty years to build it, because every time they put down a stone they had to celebrate by getting high." It was that cartoon that had started a heated discussion about the ethics of journalism. Many journalists, especially those who had their own columns, considered the sketch to be an insult to the reputation of Egypt. However, others viewed this 'insult' as a response to an academic who was addicted to drugs. This debate continued until Dr. Idris was sentenced to a prison term, fell out of the spotlight, and vanished completely from the scene. When he got out of prison after serving three years, he found that all of the doors were closed. The university had fired him and all of the research institutions had shut him out completely. Even his own family had abandoned him. His German wife had escaped shortly after the scandal broke out and had moved back home with their kids, taking most of his savings.

Mariam Gatas had not been present in Egypt during the scandal, and she had heard about it for the first time from Joseph. She was so surprised that she managed to forget about her own problem for a moment while the car was snaking through the streets towards the outskirts of Cairo and the Sayeida District. The traffic was scarce because of the weather, but when they approached the mosque of Sayeida they found themselves drowning amongst human crowds. The passages through the streets were narrow and the rain left puddles of water in a way that made the people in the streets avoid stepping in them and so they came closer to Joseph's car. Joseph turned into the street next to the police station of Sayeida and after a moment he reached the Mosque of Ahmad Ben Tolon. He turned right so that he was parallel to the fence of the huge temple in an alley that looked wide, but as he continued the alley grew narrower and narrower. Eventually it got to the point where they had to stop the car and make the rest of the expedition on foot.

When Mariam got out of the car she almost slipped in a pool of mud, but managed at the last moment not to fall. She hung her laptop bag on her right shoulder so that it hung down the left side of her body. This was something she had learned in the streets of New York to make it harder for the thieves to steal bags as they did all the time to unaware subway passengers. She looked around in suspicion as her next steps would lead her deeper and deeper into a maze of tiny alleyways. She felt the existence of curious eyes in her surroundings. She saw watching strangers who violated the fence of fear that usually surrounded the alleyways and streets in the big cities. The rain had almost come to a stop with only a light spray remaining in warning of the potential return of bad weather. Being cautious not to slip, Joseph led Mariam through an alleyway that looked like it had been constructed on a hill. Her steps were laborious as she climbed up the sticky mud, but the hardship didn't last long. Joseph quickly led her through the entrance of an old house. The entrance was similar to a cave, wafting the stench of mould. She followed him inside. Before she took her first step up the dark stairs, she ran into a large garbage can that fell over and made a loud clanking sound. A cat ran through her legs and she screamed silently, containing herself. Suddenly, one of the apartment doors swung open and out came a skinny man who eyed them with suspicion. Joseph spoke rapidly,

"Dr. Yonas Idris."

The man in the doorway pointed upstairs. Joseph thanked him and started ascending the stairs. Then he hesitated and let Mariam go in front. She climbed up the stairs sensing that the eyes of the man in the doorway were penetrating her back, but she never turned around to verify. After climbing three storeys, she suddenly found herself breathing the refreshing night air. The roof of the building was more beautiful than she had initially thought. From the eastern side the house overlooked the historical mosque of Tolon with its vast constructional extensions; and from the opposite side hanging on the horizon was the fortress of "Saladin". It appeared as if it was watching over them from afar. On the right side, the Minarets of "Sultan Hasan" Mosque, the "Refay" Mosque, and dozens of other monumental temples were adorning the view and lighting the night of Cairo like huge candles. At the end of the roof there was a tiny canopy that was covered in vines. Under the canopy lay a body that wasn't concerned with the rain or the cold. In front of the body was a smouldering vase that contained pieces of tobacco and hot coals.

Mariam followed Joseph. As they approached the canopy, the features of the reclining human body started to get clearer and clearer. He suddenly awoke, looking up to check who was paying him this visit. Then he stood up, smiling sardonically and shaking his head.

"Welcome, Journalism."

Joseph greeted the man warmly. When he started to introduce Mariam, Dr. Yonas made a theatrical gesture as if he was surprised by her existence. Kissing her hand in respect, he spoke to her in excellent French.

"Oh, it seems like your journal's level has recently improved a lot. My greeting to the young, charming lady."

Mariam was totally surprised by the gesture. She tried to withdraw her hand but Dr. Yonas's grip was tight and he was faster. She felt a shiver when she saw her hand being engulfed by his dense moustache and beard before it touched his lips gently. And when she withdrew her hand she found him smiling and saying,

"Joseph told me that you are in big trouble because of an old Pharaonic inscription. What did you do, my dear, to agitate the hornet's nest?"

*************

Despite his huge body, Dr. Yonas was able to move with ease and grace through the tiny room like a ballet dancer. As he prepared the tea, he whistled the joyful melody of Mozart's "The Magic Flute". Mariam and Joseph sat on an old couch across from him. In front of them on her laptop the familiar Windows' greeting sting floated off into the night. The pictures she had taken the day before were a little dark but they were clear. Thanks to the HD camera, she had been able to enlarge the pictures without fearing that the pixilation would lessen the quality of the image and lose the details.

"Could you please make the picture bigger?" asked Joseph, pointing to the screen.

Mariam clicked on the image and typed in a command, enlarging the image.

"A little bit to the right... yes... uh zoom in on the symbols on the left there."

The symbol was circular in nature, a sort of incomplete oval shape. The line bordering the left side was unclear and beside it was a triangle facing the sign of Ankh, which was the Pharaonic symbol of life. Mariam remembered that she had seen the same symbol before and she felt it looked strangely familiar. She spoke in a loud voice,

"I'm pretty sure I have photographed this before. Where, I don't know."

Mariam clicked on one of the icons on the desktop and opened the photo search program. Her version was the trial version which she had acquired from a friend working in the American CIA when she had participated as a photographer covering the war in Iraq. She explained her plan to Joseph:

"This program works just by using the picture files. It turns the shades and lines into numeric values and searches the memory of the computer for similar images."

"I think other programs used by the police work in the same fashion, only they use fingerprint scans," said Joseph.

"Exactly. There are other high technology programs that the American Administrations spend billions of dollars developing. These are used to search the faces of criminals and terrorists escaping from the law. Those programs can be downloaded onto surveillance cameras to track any suspicious people and alert the cops."

The program that Mariam had on her laptop was much simpler than any of these other programs; after all, it was just a trial copy for civilian use. However, it yielded the same results nonetheless. She was able to search through the thousands of pictures that she had saved on the hard drive of her laptop and access ones that matched the symbol on the artefact. Mariam was soon able to isolate the part of the image bearing the Pharaonic symbol and she pasted it into the program and ran the search. The laptop made a spinning noise as the utility searched through billions of pieces of information. A status bar appeared, indicating that the process was going to take a little more than ten minutes.

"The teaaaaaaaaaaaaaa..." called Dr. Yonas in a high, almost operatic voice, as he brought them the tray with the cups of tea and some biscuits. He looked odd. His dense beard was a mesh of little white hairs and his hair was long and silver with a small bald patch on the crown of his head. He wore a very expensive "Robe de Chambre". It was old and dirty but the brilliance of the expensive wool was still there, telling the luxurious past of the good doctor. Dr. Yonas bent down and placed the tray down next to the laptop. He examined the screen with great interest for a moment, but then laughed and turned to both of them, saying, "You are in big international trouble. Didn't I tell you - you really got into the hornet's nest."

Mariam looked at him, puzzled. This was the second time in less than five minutes that he had used this expression. Dr. Yonas gazed back at her steadily and then added, "You've got your hands on the key of secrets of the ancient City of the Sun. These secrets are able to rewrite our entire history as we know it thus far, even as far as revisiting some 'truths' that people, numbering in the billions, hold dear."

Then he sat down on the chair across from them and took a deep breath. It seemed like he was preparing himself for a long academic lecture.

\*\*\*\*\*\*\*\*\*\*

"By the end of the eighteenth century, the European civilizations had suffered a great turbulence in their own social and political systems as the Catholic Church was the only guarantor of the divine right protecting the thrones of kings and princes and providing stable ethical rules on which states and countries were built. Then came the modern ages with ethical revolutions that tore away the political power of the Catholic Church and almost tore away its religious hold as well. The eighteenth century witnessed a ferocious attack from philosophers like Voltaire, Diderot, and others on the traditional concepts of religion. Europe entered a new age: the Age of Reason. The cultural and religious legacy began to back away. New concepts started to consider the religious legacy of the Church as if it was a legend. The enlightened academic circles adopted a reasoning discipline, refusing the old beliefs and re-explaining the natural phenomenon around us in a physical way after the long reign of religious metaphysics that had dominated human consciousness for long centuries."

Mariam stared into the eyes of Dr. Yonas in shock as he was speaking. She had not realized the relationship between the complicated historical introduction with her actual problem, and when she glanced at Joseph, she found him silent. She tried to interrupt Dr. Yonas, but he motioned for her to stay silent as he continued:

"The most important rulers of Europe at that age were atheists, like Frederich the Great King of Prussia and Catherine the Second, Empress of Russia. And those rulers showed a great deal of sympathy to the philosophers of their time, but by the end of the 18th century the French Revolution had erupted with blood and violence. It cut off the head of the King of France, along with his nobles, and France was terrified by the age of terrorism. The whole continent of Europe suffered a series of wars that destroyed the throne of the Holy Roman Empire in Vienna and shook the pillars of the European thrones from Moscow to London. At that particular historical moment the European governments realized how dangerous the collapse of their religious principles could be to their own societies. They started to control the academic institutions and set limits on what was considered acceptable thought and study in a way that maintained at least a minimum level of respect to the religious principles."

At this moment Mariam could not control her temper and started to object by responding in a heated interruption: "With all due respect, Doctor, religion never contradicts what the brain is capable of. There are lots of scientists and scholars who excel in their fields - Christians, Muslims, and Jews who have never lost their faith in God. In fact, they have found proof in their sciences that led them to the pure faith that is without contradiction."

Dr. Yonas looked at her reproachfully and said, "All I am asking you to do is to be patient. Don't interrupt me until I am finished with this introduction. It's the only way you will understand what is happening to you. The problem is not in the battle between atheism and faith; the problem lies with those who insist upon determining a particular shade of faith and enforcing it to achieve their own desires in this mortal life. As the Empress of Russia, Catherine the Second (who was obviously atheist) led lots of ferocious wars against the Ottoman Sultan in pursuit of a very important, strategic goal for expanding her empire. This was of course reaching the Black Sea and assuring straight navigation in the Bosphorus Stretch. In order to achieve that, she dressed the war in religious robes and made it look like a religious crusade. In the end it looked like a war between the Christians and the Muslim Turks. It's politics, my dear... which is a dirty game that does not recognize faith nor religion but instead exploits beliefs in order to gather the masses. It's done to justify dirty goals. The rulers in Europe felt that their thrones could be threatened if the religious regime collapsed under the breakthrough of science and philosophical thought. But since the New Renaissance Age, there has always been a great debate between scientists and scholars from one side and the religious authority on the other. And scientists of physics and astronomy (like Galileo and Copernicus) rebelled against the old church mode of thinking despite the persecution they faced. In the end, for the scientific community it was a victory which the church adhered to, but the problem was that the belief of people never changed."

In the mind of Joseph there sparked a memory of an old debate that had occurred before his eyes. This debate was between his cousin Ismail and another student of the med school. This had been many years ago. Joseph had been sitting with Mariam in the cafeteria one day, waiting for Ismail to finish teaching his microbiology lab. When the lab was over and the students poured out, Ismail was late to leave. Joseph had found him exiting the room in a heated discussion with a group of religious students. Ismail had looked unusually fed up with the discussion and the argument had gotten way out of hand. Voices were raised in the corridor, making it sound more like a fight than a discussion between students and a teaching assistant. And when Ismail reached Mariam and Joseph in the cafeteria, all the bearded opponents went away except for one who looked to be the most passionate and persistent. That student was asking to be allowed to carry out a project on his own to prove the hypothesis that the microbes existing on the left wing of the fly contained anti-agents that deactivated the microbes on the right wing. When Ismail responded by saying that this hypothesis was impossible both medically and scientifically, the student said,

"May the Great God forgive you for that sin. This was a miracle we were passed down from God. You will never be a Muslim until you accept this."

"It isn't your right to take me out of Islam. How dare you? You are exceeding your limits and this discussion is over."

With lots of firmness and anger, Ismail had ended the conversation. When he sat down with Mariam and his cousin to drink a glass of lemonade, he had explained to them how a group of religious students had argued with him about the explanation of a speech delivered by the Prophet mohamad. If someone was eating and a fly landed in his dish or his cup, all he had to do to sanitize his food was to dip the opposite wing that had touched the meal because one of the wings had the disease and the other the cure. Ismail had explained to the student that whether the Great Prophet had made this statement was highly doubtful because it contradicted science, logic, and common sense. The students had responded by claiming that Ismail was a disbeliever by his refusal to accept what the prophet said. They had labelled him as a heretic...

Joseph recalled this incident while he was listening to the discussion between Dr. Yonas and Mariam. He interrupted them for the first time saying, "I think that Dr. Yonas is trying to say that there is a big difference between the pure core of the religion and the huge amount of additional commentary added later, which has become just as holy as the religion itself. For example, could you tell me why the Church stood against Galileo and Copernicus? How would it hurt the core beliefs by realizing that the earth revolved around the sun or the sun revolved around the earth so long as we recognize that God made both of them? Why did all the religious Christians believe that creation occurred only four thousand years before the birth of Jesus? After all, science has proven again and again that human beings existed on earth way before that date which the Church had arbitrarily determined... could such a discovery change the reality of true faith?"

Doctor Yonas looked at Joseph acceptingly and said, "I don't want to argue about religion or history. It was merely a brief introduction to help you understand how the Sacred Historical Protocol had been formed and how it relates to the problem that is blowing up in your face right now."

"The Sacred Historical Protocol ?"

The words sounded like an old church bell ringing in her head. They sounded omniscient, like they had echoed through the ages after originating in a dark hole of a Gothic cathedral somewhere in history.

"In the year 1765 a mysterious scientific organization formed in England. None of the historians at the time felt any need to pay attention to it, although it had a big effect on the course of history as we know it. This organization was called the Lunar Society and it was known as a club and an official society that was composed of industrialists and philosophers. They gathered regularly between 1765 and 1813 in the city of Birmingham, England. The reason why it was called the Lunar Society was because all of its members would gather when the moon was full every month. This society contained many of the most important thinkers in England: some were religious and others were doubters or atheists. This society tried to establish a set of rules that would be applied to all areas of scientific research so that no one would violate the established principles of their religion. The efforts were carried out solely by the scientists and thinkers who were never privileged with support from the government until the earthquake of the French Revolution shook the pillars of Europe's thrones. After that the European governments drew attention to the importance of religion in stabilizing the political and ethical aspects of society. The English Royal Society (which is the highest scientific society in Britain) started to adopt this ethical commitment by not letting science violate the principles of religion. After the defeat of Napoleon during the Battle of Waterloo, the French academics joined as well and most of the European and American institutions followed suit in adhering to this protocol. Not only that, but the Ottoman Empire also participated in adapting this protocol for the reason that the main religious principles in Christianity are similar to the ones found in Islam."

Miriam interrupted: "This doesn't make any sense. If you claim that the major scientific societies in the free world committed to not violating the religious principles, then the European and American scientific principles of the 19th and 20th century violated this protocol, starting with Darwin's theory of evolution and ending with Hawking's theory about the beginning of the universe." Mariam asked herself whether Joseph had brought her to a mad scientist who had destroyed his brain with a serious hashish addiction.

Dr. Yonas smiled, looking at Mariam as if he was looking at her thoughts.

"Actually, this protocol was adopted by the governments but it wasn't enforced by law. The governments were able to provide financial and intangible support for those who agreed with the protocol and withheld it from those who refused. However, they were never able to carry out inquisitions with the opposition like the Catholic Church did during the Middle Ages. Implemental sciences such as physics, biology, and chemistry in all their forms were derived from this with the exception of one science."

Dr. Yonas fell silent to see if his listeners were captivated. Indeed they were.

"The disciplines of archaeology and all the known history of the East have been committed to the protocol in the upmost way not to violate the existing stories in the holy books."

"Do you mean that this is the reason why the protocol is called the Sacred Historical Protocol?" Joseph asked with great interest.

"Yes! A lot of factors played a big part in this commitment, as excavations with the intention of finding monuments is an expensive job which can't be done without the support of governments. Also, the result of these excavations is not like looking for gold or oil, which in the end you can sell as a good. Excavations, as you know, lead to nothing but finding old information that serve no use to anyone except for researchers of history."

"How can you say this? Lots of excavations in the name of monuments lead to finding priceless golden treasures!" retorted Joseph.

Dr. Yonas responded by emphasizing the last words out of Joseph's mouth, "Priceless treasures... the price of gold comes only when you melt it down and convert it into coins, but what would be the value in something that is forbidden to be traded? The word priceless means it is extremely valuable, but at the same time it is utterly worthless. To add to this, the golden treasures only represent a miniscule percentage of success in excavations anyhow. Many times pieces of stone or papyrus are more valuable then tons of gold; that is why excavations done in the name of monuments are never carried out unless there is a financier who is ready to pay lots of money without getting anything in return.

That is why archaeological excavation is a science that is dependent on the generosity of the academic institutions which are able to put up the money for research that has no tangible return. Those responsible for the Sacred Historical Protocol were always keen to be the primary sources of finance and granting and controlling the academic institutions themselves. That is how the protocol of sacred history began controlling the entire process of archaeological excavations and forcing the workers in this field to adhere to the rule that the findings will never contrast or disprove the stories in the holy books."

Joseph tried to object, but a sudden buzzing came from Mariam's laptop. She remarked with excitement: "The search is finished."

Dr. Yonas looked to her inquiringly and Joseph explained, "Mariam felt like she has seen this symbol before and that is why she has been searching through her photo archive to find out when she photographed it previously."

The three heads peered at the laptop screen which displayed a couple of photographs that Mariam had shot last August. In the photographs was an empty office, and at first it appeared that there was no connection between the symbol and what they were looking at. Dr. Yonas stared at the picture, wide-eyed, and suddenly his face went pale. He turned to Mariam and looked at her in disbelief.

*************

In silence a four by four jeep with tinted glass windows rolled slowly through the narrow streets of the Alsayeda district. The driver, despite his foreign features, appeared to know the area well and after a short while the car stopped at the fence of the Ahmad Mosque. The engine was shut off along with the headlights and it seemed like a predator had closed his eyes, taking a nap before the big hunt.

Jakov Banshiev looked at the Blackberry that was fastened to his dashboard and smiled. The target had been located and he was just waiting for the green light to carry out the mission. He didn't like it when he was told to wait while on the job. He had been told not to call the mark until the order was given. The leadership wanted to make sure that none of the information was leaked on the internet or Facebook before it gave him the green light to move in and silence the target forever. In the darkness of the car the only light was the faint glow from the Blackberry which had a GPS application opened. It was showing a complete map of the whole area with all the details, alleyways, and houses. A red glow on the map identified a spot roughly 200 metres from the car. This was of course the prey, who was unaware that the hunter was waiting.

*********

The picture that appeared on Mariam's laptop was of an empty office, and on the left wall of the room there was a frame bearing Pharaonic symbols. When Mariam maximized the details of the symbol it matched the symbol she was looking for perfectly.

"I know this office well. How did you photograph it?" Dr. Yonas asked seriously.

Looking at the file bearing the image, Mariam hit the right button on the mouse to expand the menu. She searched the file's history.

"This picture dates back to last August. This is part of a collection of photographs I took in the office of Dr. Gamal Omran while I was covering his sudden death that shocked the academic circles."

"You mean his murder, not his death."

"There was no crime. Dr. Gamal died naturally due to a sudden heart attack after a small fire in his apartment when he tripped over the hose of his stove's propane tank."

Joseph recalled the accident, as he had participated in covering the story. When the body of Dr. Gamal was found in his apartment in the "Al Dokee" district, he had second degree burns on the lower part of his body. The coroner's report had showed that the burns had not caused his death and had also determined that he had not been asphyxiated by the gas leaking from the hose, as the propane tank in his apartment was almost empty. The leakage had lasted only a few minutes, which is why the fire hadn't spread to the rest of the apartment. The report had drawn the conclusion that Dr. Gamal might have had a heart attack caused by the shock of seeing the fire consuming him. Some of the students of Dr. Gamal doubted this scenario greatly, claiming that highly important manuscripts had vanished from his office. He had devoted the last five years of his life to very important research, but not a shred of this work had been found on the scene. The police had closed the investigation, considering it an accident as there was no evidence of foul play.

"Doctor, please don't tell me that you honestly believe the rumours on the blogs that Gamal was murdered by foreign secret intelligence to silence him," Joseph asked Dr. Yonas sarcastically.

Dr. Yonas took a deep breath and his face showed sadness. He replied, "Unfortunately... violating the rules of the Sacred Historical Protocol always results in violence... have you ever heard of the Curse of the Pharaohs? This interesting story has always been told by the media whenever a scholar or an archaeologist looking for Pharaonic monuments died in mysterious ways. The fact is that this superstition was invented to cover up lots of similar murders. Excavating for monuments and revealing ancient secrets is hard and dangerous work, and so a mysterious death is always the punishment awarded to those who cross the line by revealing the secrets."

Dr. Yonas went silent for a moment, and then he said, smiling, "Did you know that hashish is the only thing that saved me from sharing the same fate as Dr. Gamal?"

Joseph and Mariam looked at him inquiringly.

He continued, "Actually some researchers in the field of ancient history, not all of them, are exposed to the same dangers. Some of them are just adventurers looking for fame who never have any credibility to back them, and the ones responsible for the protocol do not pay any attention to these types. They are dealt with as if they were legend makers, like those who hypothesized about the mystic power of the pyramids or the interventionist alien theory. These kind of researchers never disturb the protocol and they do not affect serious research. The real threat is when a credible researcher provides a new point of view or a study that crosses the scientific principles of history that were enforced by the protocol. In such a case it becomes a danger. Interference with these rousers is a must, even if it is at the cost of destroying reputations or going as far as murder. Usually murder is the last option because there are thousands of ways to force the rebel researchers to reconsider their opinions. There is always temptation with lucrative positions in international institutions and generous funding for their research, excavations, and restorations, but if all these temptations do not work, then it is time to look at the researcher's weaknesses like his financial situation, his sexual behaviour, or his personal relationships - anything that could be used to create a scandal."

He smiled sadly for the second time.

"Hashish saved my neck. It was a weak point in my personal behaviour that made them able to destroy my life and discredit me. But a character like Dr. Gamal Omran was devoid of any weaknesses. He was honest, he wasn't greedy, and he had no interest in any temptations. He remained brave before any threats. That is why he left them with no other options except murder."

"Murder... murder! You use this term too much. This isn't the mafia we are talking about. This is an international academic institution, 'supposedly', which is trying to dominate the course of scientific research in history," said Mariam, shaking her head.

Joseph expanded on her thought, saying, "Doctor, you are talking about scientists and academics who have principles and who are religious trying to ban everything that contradicts the stories in the holy texts. This makes it hard to believe that they would resort to murder and scandal; after all, they have a pure goal."

"Dear Joseph, the whole protocol of sacred history was about to vanish by the end of the nineteenth century as some sciences had started to take a free course in research, even if it was contradictory to the preconceived beliefs of religion. For example, sciences like anthropology rebuilt the ancient explanations found in the Torah. Before they were known as Negroes, Mongolians, and Caucasians, the races were named after the sons of Noah: Sam, Ham, and Japheth."

Mariam shook her head slowly as if she was attempting to comprehend.

"It's true. According to the Torah, all people are the descendants of the sons of Noah - those who survived the flood. The Torah also tells us that while Noah was asleep, he had exposed himself. His son Ham saw this scene and he had laughed at his father. He had joked about this with his brothers. The other son, Sam, had brought a robe and covered the genitals of his father without looking. When Noah woke up and found out what had happened, he cursed Ham by calling him a slave to his brothers for the rest of his descendancy. This story was exploited and used as an ethical base for slave traders to rationalize shipping millions of Africans to the Americas for slave labour. This was done without any pain in their consciences, despite the fact that most of them were religious Christians, because they believed that Africans were the descendants of Ham, the son of Noah. Their skin was black because of the curse that Noah had placed on his son."

"Yeah, but Christianity is innocent from this racial discrimination of human beings. Jesus came with the messages of love, unity, and brotherhood for all of mankind," said Mariam with enthusiasm.

Dr. Yonas nodded in agreement and added, "Yes, of course. I am not talking about the message of Jesus nor the religious books. I am talking about the explanation that groups of people made to justify the deviation from the message of the prophets. This deviation simply guaranteed that they would make huge financial revenues. Europe gained incredible financial growth over three centuries, and even in the twentieth century lots of politicians used the same explanations and terms to support their political agenda. Have you ever heard of Robert Byrd?"

Mariam looked at Dr. Yonas, trying to remember this name that sounded so familiar.

"Ahh... you mean the famous American senator. He was the oldest member of the senate."

"Yes. Do you know that in the year 1964, during the peak of the African American struggle to end the apartheid and gain civil rights, this senator stood in the middle of the senate holding the Torah and reciting the story of Noah as a justification to keep the apartheid?"

"So what I understand from your words is that anthropology in its beginnings was totally influenced by the Torah, and that is why people were divided into these three categories of Samets, Hamets, and Japheths. And when science revolted it rebuilt its foundation on that irrational classification of races, but they used more rational terms like Caucasian, Negro, and Mongolian?"

"Yes. In a short time the other disciplines such as physics and biology were rebuilt on the same rules. Darwin led a huge revolution against the old beliefs in the middle of the nineteenth century, but particularly with a discipline like history lots of occurrences happened that saved the Sacred Historical Protocol from dying out. With the growth of Zionism in the world, politicians in the Western world played on the religious legacy to justify the idea of planting a new state in the middle of the Arabic area. The Bible started to be an ethical and religious base for planting the idea of the state of Israel: 'For your breed I give this land from the river of Egypt to the big river.' This was the divine pact for the Promised Land that God made more than once, just as He had done in Genesis to Abraham and Jacob. Mythology and all the legends became a new moving power for the most important political decisions in the modern age, and any attempts to criticize or re-examine the writings of the Torah and how they fit into history were looked upon as a huge heresy that doubted the divine attributes of the Jewish people. This ideology became the basis for all international policy in the twentieth century. Hitler persecuted the gypsies as well as the Jews in an attempt to wipe them out, but no one in the Western societies accepted the idea of creating a separate state for the gypsies. The reason was that the gypsies did not have a divine promise to their own holy land anywhere. There are still many people who use this religious legacy to boost the enthusiasm of religious people towards accepting the idea of the battle of Armageddon, a battle that is really about good overcoming evil in a final bout and paving the way for a new world. And if you were to see how many times the word 'Armageddon' was searched on Google after September 11th, you would be surprised. It was searched more times than Al-Qaeda, Osama, or even New York."

Mariam felt her patience was wearing thin with these harebrained conspiracy theories of this drug-addicted professor. It appeared that the drugs had destroyed his brain and made him extremely paranoid. She was provoked by how the holy books were described as vague legends and she cried out in a nervous way, pointing to the laptop, "For God's sake, doctor, what do you see in these pictures that might reform all of history or agitate those whom you think are responsible for proving the literal accuracy of those books?"

Dr. Yonas ignored her aggressive, sarcastic tone and answered seriously and calmly: "You, my dear, cannot see the trouble your picture could cause if it fell in the hands of one of these serious researchers. It opens up a big door towards the City of the Sun, the one that the ancient Egyptians knew as 'IWN' or 'IWONO', which the ancient Greeks later called 'Heliopolis'. This is the same place where the ancient civilization of Egypt came into existence in the pre-dynastic era. The priests of that city were responsible for all of the secrets of a mysterious civilization that preceded all that we know about ancient Egypt in a way that can rewrite all of that history from scratch."

The eyes of Dr. Yonas were shimmering brilliantly. Wide-eyed he asked, "...Do you have any idea why there is no mention of any great prophets of the holy texts in all that we know from Egypt? The reason lies simply in the way that Egyptology has been formed. This discipline started humbly at the beginning of the nineteenth century during the French military campaign led by Napoleon in Egypt. This was actually the same time when the Sacred Historical Protocol was at the peak of its power and influence. It is not a coincidence that the Rosetta Stone, which bore the answers to the mystery of the hieroglyphic writings, was about to cause a bloody war between the English and the French. After both parties agreed to a treaty in Alexandria, the English knew about an old stone that the French scientists had discovered that bore inscriptions of three different languages, including hieroglyphics and Greek. This led to comparisons between the two inscriptions which shaped the way we understand the ancient Egyptian language. The British army refused to let the French leave Egypt without handing over the precious stone. When the French didn't want to comply, a war was imminent until the French finally surrendered at the last minute. The British seized the Rosetta Stone that to this day is housed in the British Museum. Now you may ask what could be the importance of such a stone, especially if it had been poised to provoke a war between two civilized nations.

"Egyptology as a modern science was established on three lies. They were enforced at the beginning of the nineteenth century by the Sacred Historical Protocol. The first lie was that we call the ancient Egyptians Pharaohs and we believe that all of their kings were called this way (the equivalent to Caesar in Rome). This is totally untrue. The second lie was that the Egyptian civilization began in 3200 BC. And the third lie was that the ancient Egyptian language never changed over 3,000 years (until the time that the Rosetta Stone was created in 200 BC). The dictionary provided by the Rosetta Stone was able to translate any Egyptian texts starting at the beginning of the pyramids up until the stone was written. However, the Rosetta Stone was simply an artefact which was written in 198 BC during the Ptolemaic period. The Egyptologists supposed that the Egyptian language that was spoken then would be the same that the ancient Egyptians had used to communicate with 3,000 years prior when the pyramids were built. Yet this is extremely contradictory with the simplest facts about languages, because languages tend to evolve and change according to the expressions that come from other languages and interactions with foreign vocabularies. To understand what I mean, just look at the English language today compared to the language spoken in England 1,000 years ago."

Mariam's look had turned from impatience to a sudden blank daze. Somewhere in her head a sound was repeating itself from the depths of her memory. She recalled a trip which had been organized by the medical school to the monumental places in Egypt. She was extremely excited for this trip. Although she belonged to a big family which had originated in Southern Egypt, she hadn't visited the monuments of her native land. This trip was the starting point of her relationship with Ismail, who was accompanying the group because of his position as an instructor at the university. In one of the visits to the Temple of Dendera, Dr. Saeed Thabit, the professor at the med school and the head of the Society of History Lovers, was explaining some astonishing revelations about the temple's ceiling. The ancient Egyptians had painted a huge circle on the ceiling that represented the sky. It was divided into twelve sections, each one representing a different Zodiac sign. When he had finished his explanation he had caught his breath and said,

"This ceiling represents powerful evidence that the ancient Egyptian civilization is far more ancient than what the Egyptologists claim. This temple dates back to 2500 BC, which implies that the astrological studies of the Egyptians, as knowledgeable as they were at this time, in fact started thousands of years before that date. Maybe this is the reason that the temple was subject to a conspiracy to steal its ceiling and move it to France where the original is exhibited to this day. What you are seeing now is just a replica made of stucco that was applied in the twentieth century."

Joseph noticed the blank expression in Mariam's eyes. She seemed to not be listening to anything that Dr. Yonas was saying. Joseph raised his hands and waved his arms in front of her face.

"Hey, Mariam, are you still there?"

Mariam awoke from her daze and felt a little self-conscious. She replied, trying to hide her shyness, "Uh oh no - Nothing.... I was just thinking about a trip I took to the temple of Dendera in the South of Egypt where I heard similar things to what Dr. Yonas is saying."

For the second time, the eyes of Dr. Yonas widened with a brilliant twinkle and he smiled, saying, "Oh, Dendera Temple. For sure you were thinking of the ceiling of the temple that was transferred to France under mysterious conditions in the year 1821. Did you know that King Louis XVIII funded half the cost of the delivery of the ceiling out of his own pocket while the French government covered the rest? And as soon as the ceiling arrived in Paris a big intellectual battle began between the remaining philosophers who were pro-revolution and the conservatives who were pro-reality. There was a book written by a French thinker called DuBois in which he described religious beliefs as being born at the same time as the agricultural societies. The principles were created around the harvests. Those societies were depending mainly on weather conditions of rains and floods, and for that they began to use astrological observations. DuBois believed that the beginning of astrological knowledge would have started in and around 12000 BC, which would make the history of ancient Egypt a lot deeper than the information that the Sacred Historical Protocol had provided. At the time this book sparked a huge debate between the religious leaders (those who found it contradictory with the Torah, dating back to Adam at around 4000 BC) and the philosophers. Thus, the book provoked an intellectual storm between the pro-church and the large number of opposing forces of the French revolution. Seizing the ceiling of the Dendera Temple and transporting it to Paris is one of the procedures that were carried out by the ones responsible for the Sacred Historical Protocol. They did this in order to form the ancient Egyptian history in their own way, similar to how they employed spies and agents in all the legal and illegal antiquity markets over the last two centuries. This was done to control all the factors surrounding documents or discoveries that may pose a threat to the sanctity of the protocol. The same thing happened in the first half of the twentieth century in Nag Hammadi, Egypt when a roll of papyrus bearing the oldest gospel was discovered. That is why it was shipped immediately to America where it remains today, banned from publishing or scientific research. The same thing happened in Jordan when the Dead Sea scrolls were discovered and seized in the same fashion and met the same end."

The historical information was spewing out of the mouth of Dr. Yonas in a way that was typical of a conspiracy theorist. Joseph noticed that Mariam had placed her head between her hands and she was breathing loudly, whispering to herself...

"My head is about to explode!"

With the instinct of an old lecturer, Dr. Yonas felt that his audience was beginning to get distracted and lose focus. He slapped his knees with his big, coarse palms and stood up exclaiming, "How about a cup of tea in the Tai style? Now I will introduce you to Dr. Yonas' secret method of activity."

He winked looking at Joseph and said, "I'm going to make you a cup of tea but not like any you have ever had before."

Joseph laughed aloud because he understood the trick and was about to respond, but he couldn't find the words to continue the joke without hurting Dr. Yonas's feelings. He looked over at Mariam, who still had her head in her hands. She looked at him with eyes full of tears and said,

"I need some fresh air. I feel like I can't breathe."

\*\*\*\*\*\*\*\*\*\*

Outside the storm was strong as if it was regaining its power to strike again. The rain had stopped but the dense black clouds were obscuring the usual starry Cairo night. From far in the distance the lightning flashes could be seen, threatening the coming of another round. The fences of the mosque of Ahmad Ben Tolon looked like ghosts guarding a legendary fortress because of the weird design which the Tolon's architect had taken from the ancient sign of Ankh. This was the same Pharaonic sign from which Christianity had taken its cross. As a result, the fences looked like an endless number of Ankhs holding hands together on guard.

Once they exited the room of Dr. Yonas to the open roof, they felt the cold air on their faces. Joseph blew into his fists to warm himself. When he looked at Mariam he found her silent and shaking in the darkness. When he held her hands they felt as cold as ice cream, but in the same way soft and delicious and dense to the touch. He raised her hands to his lips. They were wet with tears. He blew into them warm breaths and then kissed them in kindness. Mariam was surprised by the gesture. Her feelings were turbulent inside of her. She exclaimed, trying to withdraw her hands from his grasp,

"Joseph, what are you doing?"

Joseph began to stutter a little. It seemed like his gesture had been unconscious. Immediately he started to sweat. The beads of sweat began to carve paths on his forehead and on the back of his neck. He felt the blood rushing to his face and stinging him in the cheeks. Whether it was the blood of shame or excitement, he did not know, but he tried hard to pronounce the next sentence without stammering. He had lost many years of his life because he had not been brave enough to keep up with these beautiful moments, the ones that left him paralyzed and speechless.

"Mariam, maybe this is not the right time, but I want you to know something. I want you to know that I would never let anyone hurt you as long as I have a beating heart in my chest."

Her heart was bursting with joy like never before, and she smiled. She was flooded with memories that took her back to long years ago with Joseph, continuous scenes that passed before her eyes. These were scenes that she had thought about before; however, she had never understood them until now. She could see the past now with her photographic eye. She realized that in every one of these 'pictures' Joseph had always been in the background, trying to shy away from the focus. She looked deeply in his eyes and found them shimmering with a light of kindness. This was the look that had always been there in her pictures and memories. She hadn't seen it before because her focus had always been on Ismail.

"Joseph... I...."

"I am sorry Mariam. This is an unsuitable time... but..." He stammered a little but then added, "I want you to know that you will never be alone, ever, from now on."

"That's not it at all, Joseph. I am so thankful to have you. I don't know what I would have done if you hadn't been there during all those hard times... but..."

She kept silent, remembering her few cold meetings with Joseph since her return to Cairo.

"Why have I always had this feeling that you were ignoring me since I returned from London? I felt like my problems with your aunt might have..."

Joseph smiled in remembering his aunt, Ismail's mother, and how she spoke negatively about Mariam. She had always found Mariam responsible for the death of her son. She believed that their marriage had been a curse that had gotten Joseph into trouble. She also believed very deeply that her son would not have wanted to go to London unless he had wanted to escape from his family and their harassments that were constant during their life in Egypt.

"My aunt is a good woman, but circumstances never allowed her the chance to get to know you better. She is obsessed with the idea that you are a foreigner with an American passport and that at any moment you could kidnap Adam and Sarah and escape to America."

Mariam knew very well that her mother-in-law's obsession with her grandchildren was the sole reason she had seized the custody rights of Adam and Sarah and enforced strict visiting hour conditions. She took it to the extreme, even so far as hiring a private driver to escort the children to and from school. She had told Mariam that the children were Muslims and the court would never allow them to be under her custody because Mariam was a Christian. Mariam had never consulted a lawyer to find out whether this was right or wrong. She had simply given up custody of her children because she had wanted to keep the last shred of connection that she had to the family of her late husband. When she had returned from London to settle down in Egypt and be near the kids, she had been afraid to impose an ultimatum on the kids for fear that they would be torn between two different feelings of belonging - to their grandmother and to their mother. Two different kinds of love were able to gather the children and not tear them apart. Even the issue of religion was never a contradictory point between her and Ismail. The children of Ismail should bear his faith in the same way that they bore his name. She was happy that the belief that they shared was not of religion but a deep faith in love and understanding that Ismail and herself believed in.

"Kidnap my kids? Could a mother kidnap her own children? I tried to satisfy her in all possible ways, but she was always..."

"I know, Mariam. Try and be forgiving of her. Someday all this will be water under the bridge."

Taking a deep breath, Joseph felt as if he was suddenly cured from the serious chronic disease of the tongue that had hindered him from saying everything that he felt in his heart whenever he looked at Mariam.

"Ismail was not just my cousin, he was my older brother too and my lifelong friend with whom I was raised. So I buried my feelings for you ever since the moment he told me he liked you. I built up a huge wall and behind it I put all my secrets. I secured it with 100 locks and keys. I forbid myself from even touching the burning place inside me."

Turbulent feelings were controlling the heart of Mariam. Worry... Happiness... Longing... Fear... Pessimism. Among all of these contrasting feelings there was one that was shining brilliantly through the fog. She was grateful for Joseph being there in these hard moments. For the first time in a long time she felt like she wasn't alone against the world, this world that had brought her a cadaver covered in blood and placed it in her apartment. This cadaver was strangling her with guilt of a crime in the first degree. It was sentencing her for life.

She wanted to smile, but she couldn't. She forced a silent grin while she peered out on the minarets of Cairo.

"Joseph, I don't know what to do. I can't see the end of this trouble."

"Believe me, Mariam, there is a light at the end of every tunnel. Don't ever think that you are weak and that others can mess up your life and control you."

"We don't know how far their reaches of power extend. We don't even know who they are!"

"You have been away from Egypt for a long time and you have forgotten how things operate around here. However powerful these people might be, there are always honest ones waiting to help us. The truth is that you were with me all day long and I will testify to this. I have lots of friends on the force that can help us. Also, the Blackberry and the picture on it is physical proof that you were blackmailed. Even Dr. Yonas can help us with his testimony. Together we can challenge those murderers."

Mariam thought for a moment. Joseph's plan seemed imaginary to her. He was picking a fight with an invisible opponent. He was challenging a physical proof in a crime with the testimony of a washed up university professor. His connections with the constables weren't a comfort either, as they didn't extend past friendship. It seemed like Joseph was reading her silence and hearing her thoughts, as he quickly responded:

"I know well that this isn't enough… but don't be afraid. I also have lots of connections with human rights organizations all over the world. The most critical task now is that we start uploading the pictures on the internet. Publishing the truth on the largest scale will be our most valuable ally. I will leave you for a moment and get my laptop from the car with my list of contacts and email addresses. This is the most important weapon in our next steps."

Mariam did not feel comfortable with the idea of Joseph leaving her. She felt very safe in his presence. She tried to object and she discovered that her hands were still in his grasp. She found him raising them to his mouth in order to give them a quick kiss. Then he turned around and moved into the darkness that led to the roof exit. He left her paralyzed to the extent that she almost forgot to breath. She found herself sighing.

✺✺✺✺✺✺✺✺✺

Mariam raised her head to gaze at the night sky, receiving the sprays of light rain. The darkness was like one mass, extending to an absolute abyss. There were no borders between land and sky, just a few glimmering lights among houses and minarets as if they were stars which had migrated to the land, leaving the sky dark and silent. The silence was interrupted by the light vibration from her mobile in her pocket. For a moment she thought it was the cursed Blackberry, but then she recognized the voice of the Canadian singer Celine Dion,

*Every night in my dreams.*

*I see you. I feel you.*

*That is how I know you go on.*

She waited a moment before taking the mobile out of her pocket because she liked the song, but when she looked at the screen she hesitated a little bit and declined the call. It was her father calling from America. Over the past two years her dad had tried many times to contact her by sending her messages via post and email, but she had never responded. She knew in her core that Ismail had been murdered and the only one she suspected was her father, her father who had never forgiven her marriage to a Muslim against his will. She remembered his threats when she had declared the marriage to him. His Southern Egyptian anger had turned into a hot lava that spewed from his mouth and eyes. The first eight years of her marriage had passed in the shadows completely void of her father. He had never tried to contact her even after she had given birth to Adam. Ismail had insisted that she contact him because he knew how much she loved her dad and how painful her father's silence had been for her, but Dr. Gatas had received the news of the birth of his first grandson with coldness. He had hung up on his daughter and left her to retreat into the arms of her husband, who tried like usual to find an excuse for this harsh reaction.

Dr. Gatas had finally contacted her on the terrible day when she was exiting the sterile morgue in London. That day her tears were mirrors of a horrible sight... the cold body of her husband. How could her father have known what had happened unless he had taken some part in it? He had tried to give his condolences, but she had screamed at him over the phone line:

"You murdered my husband and now you want to participate in the funeral!?"

A few days later he had come to London in hopes of reconciling, but she had refused to see him. She had left London and returned to Iraq searching for that Baghdadian death that was roaming the streets. Even death itself refused to oblige her. Death had always had its own cryptic sense of humour and refused to see anyone on their terms.

The cell phone rang incessantly, but she shook her head in stubborn determination and silenced Celine Dion as she had done many times before. She sighed. Suddenly she heard a sound behind her that sounded like the echo of her sigh.

"Welcome back, Dr. Yonas. Is the tea ready?"

She turned around and heard something in her ear that resembled a hissing viper.

\*\*\*\*\*\*\*\*\*\*\*

Jakov Banshiev had not expected any resistance from Mariam. He stood behind her in the darkness, obscured from her sight. He seemed to be enjoying the look of fear in her posture. Her reaction was much faster than he had expected. In no time he found her completing her turn around followed by a lateral kick (Yoko Giri Kiaji). It connected with his face and immediately she went into a defensive stance.

After a few moments, when Mariam was reciting her last prayer, she felt a darkness crawling towards her consciousness and then complete paralysis. She felt a flow of blood from the back of her head that was spreading across the roof. At this moment she was praying because she felt like she had done all she could. She felt like she had resisted well and had almost succeeded at beating her murderer. She was surprised by her body's quick, almost instinctual reaction to the situation, and what it did to her attacker. As soon as she heard him breathing behind her, she had realized that she had heard these sounds before in the phone call on the cursed Blackberry. Her body had moved and reacted unconsciously with the Yoko Giri Kiaji. Her old Japanese Karate master had taught her well. She was never to let her thoughts interfere with her reactions. The body can always fight and win on its own as long as it has the motivation. Hard training always makes the instincts of survival prevail over rational thinking. After all, thinking was the only thing that could paralyze the body and hinder its take off...

...But there must have been a trace of thought in her mind while she had been getting ready for the next move. She had seen her opponent stunned from the force of the kick and from the surprise. She had felt that she had to end the confrontation as quickly as possible but, because of a fraction of a second, she was late in executing the punch of Ora Zuki to the throat of her mysterious enemy. She had wanted the punch to end the ordeal, but a fraction of a second had cost her a lot. She had felt a terrible electrical shock running through her body just before she hit the ground in a dull thud.

While her mind fought a coma, she could hear heavy footsteps approaching. Then there was a yellow light omitting from a taser right before it struck the body of Dr. Yonas who was exiting his hut with his tray of tea. The huge body of Dr. Yonas hit the floor and she heard the sound of shattering glass all over the place. The pieces from the tea set had scattered everywhere. She could smell the fragrance of the tea.

Jakov Banshiev assumed the standby position, panting after this unexpected and undesired fight. He listened carefully to see if the sound of the struggle had caught the attention of any curious neighbours, but the surrounding windows looked like closed eyes whose lids were keeping the tenants tucked away inside - the ones who were lucky to have escaped the storm.

Jakov walked around the roof for a moment, and then he entered Dr. Yonas' hut looking for anyone else.

"Great; nobody here."

He left the hut, pacified his breathing with his inhaler, and wiped off the blood from his nose. He stood and examined the scene. He was trying to evaluate the situation and find his next move.

\*\*\*\*\*\*\*\*\*\*

The liberal nature of Massachusetts made it one of the states in favour of the Democratic Party. It always disagreed with the policies of the Republicans with respect to their tight relationship with the right, which was strongly growing in America. Yet the state's history reflected obvious contrasts with its electoral results. The capital of the state was Boston, a city that bore a religious name meaning the city of the baptized. Boston was founded by a group of English pilgrims who had escaped prosecution in Europe in hopes of finding religious freedom in the beginning of the seventeenth century. The state was the stage for witch hunts in its early years, especially in Salem where Arthur Miller's play was inspired by the many witch burnings that had taken place there. The power of religion was so strong that it forced the type of extremist values that had been prevalent in Europe in the seventeenth century. This also polluted the history of the church with numerous trials and persecution of 'heretics'.

Dr. Gatas used to think about this old history while driving through the streets of Boston towards the Charles River where the town of Cambridge lay. Being home to several prestigious universities, Cambridge was the pride of the city. It was strange to see the contrasts between the scientific institutions, which elevated the human brain to higher planes; and the Sacred Historical Protocol, which implemented restraints on scientific research dating back to the Middle Ages whenever any violations to the red lines of the protocol occurred. Any violations were dealt with by impalement and burning. Two contrasts of this sort could not be found anywhere else except for Boston.

Dr. Yahia stopped his car right in front of the huge building of HSA. He asked the driver to wait for him and got out of the car. Before ascending the marble stairs of the luxurious building, he paused for a moment, took his cell phone out of his coat pocket, and pressed the redial button. He brought the cell phone on his ear to listen to the dialing on the other end with no answer.

*********

In the backless *soirée* dress, barefoot and with red exhausted eyes, Hannah Gabriel greeted the morning from the confines of her office. She felt lucky that no one had seen her in her present state, as her appearance would not be acceptable for the morning work atmosphere. The first and only conclusion that might pop into the head of anyone who saw her would be that she had drank too much last night and snuck away to her office for a hot night with a co-worker or worse, a boss. Fortunately, Hacky Hannah's office, which was attached to John Howard's office, was relatively far from the lecture halls and classrooms of the anthropology wing.

Life in the classrooms started relatively later than it did on the administrative side of the university, which was still asleep. Most of the employees had not yet shown up. Maybe their lateness was due to last night's lavish party in the hall. But Hannah and John Howard hadn't slept, being burdened by a load of work and what seemed like endless correspondences.

Two hours ago Hannah had been about to collapse. It wasn't because of the workload or relentless tasks that John Howard (whose nerves had been shot the whole night) was assigning to her. In fact, Hannah was suffering from a strangling sensation that made her feel as if she was making a grave error. This was a feeling that caused a pain in her throat whenever she was trying to swallow, leaving her with a tightness in the chest and an itch under the skin. It was as if a small mouse was messing about under her ribs and a silent noise was repeating itself over and over again under her skull. This was her conscious, that hidden organ that we cannot touch whenever it inflicts us with pain.

Hacky Hannah was used to going through the firewalls and minefields that were apparent in any mainframe. She was well-practiced with going through any virtual door and being able to find a way in. These things were not a big deal for a professional hacker. But when she entered the website that Howard had asked her to penetrate, she had found a mine that exploded in her face. It was called Dr. Yahia Gatas. Finding his name shook the credibility of what she was doing. She was now hacking into the personal accounts of the daughter of the man who had saved her life. This was the man whose hands were responsible for giving her new life on the operating table. Dr. Gatas had created her a new heart from scratch. She recalled how she had lived over 20 years of her life like a semi-paraplegic in her bed, expecting death every night and waking up every morning to the miracle of life. All the doctors had assured her that a cure was impossible, but then she had managed to beat the world champion of chess in a charity match. After the media had told her story as a model of challenging illness and fighting for life, Dr. Yahia Gatas had called and invited her for a medical examination. He had received her with a parental warmth and had promised to devote his research to finding a surgical cure for her condition. He had revitalized the hope in her heart. All he asked was for her to hang on and continue fighting. After two years of research and hanging on, Hannah was in an operating room, putting her life in the hands of the good doctor. Then the miracle came true.

The deeper Hannah went into Mariam Gatas's Facebook page and email account, the more she felt like she was betraying her heart - a heart which might still bear the fingerprints of Dr. Yahia Gatas. Each time Professor Howard asked her to conduct more searches and violate his privacy further, the guilty feeling doubled. She knew that Professor Howard was doing something for a greater, nobler aim. She understood the general idea behind the Sacred Historical Protocol and she agreed that the prophets' stories and sacred texts should not be messed with by the hands of fame seekers, treasure hunters, or archaeologists. Yet the lines of the protocol that Hannah had imagined seemed to be blurred. It all seemed like a bunch of academic pressure to her now, practiced by those who were responsible for the history and archaeology departments in the universities and international museums to support a particular view. The methods they used for that purpose seemed soft and simple, such as throwing money in the form of grants at history researchers who had adopted the required point of view and banning funds from anyone else. But what could be the relationship between Mariam Gatas and the Sacred Historical Protocol to have Professor Howard so interested? Mariam Gatas was not a researcher in history or archaeology, and it didn't seem, from her personal accounts, that she had any relation with those matters. Every time Howard pushed her to run more searches, the more Hannah felt like a sinner. In one of her moments of guilt, Hannah, pushed by curiosity, decided to hack Professor Howard's computer to have a quick look for anything that might say more about his sudden interest in Mariam. At first she was surprised by how difficult it was to hack into his computer. She encountered specialized anti-spyware and firewalls that should have belonged to a high ranking secret agent, not just some university professor. Hannah recalled her previous experience in hacking the CIA server to gain access, and when she applied these actions to Professor Howard's computer, she was overcome by surprise to find a complete network of relationships with academic institutions and cooperating secret intelligence agencies in different countries. These connections seemed totally contradictory to the life of a noble scientific researcher. Why would Professor Howard be connected to this dark underworld of secret agents and organized criminal gangs? What could be the reason that could cause a respectful academic institution to hire murderers and smuggling gangs and pay huge amounts in bribes for mysterious missions? The protocol used the corruption in the Middle East to control any archaeological findings.

Hacky Hannah knew that Professor John Howard believed in the principles of the Sacred Historical Protocol to the extent of doing whatever necessary to preserve them, but she never imagined that he could be involved in something like murder for the sake of this goddamned protocol.

*\*\*\*\*\*\*\*\*\*\**

On the rain-soaked roof Jakov Banshiev stood panting as he re-evaluated the entire situation and remade his plan according to these new happenings. The crime scene was a mess with shattered glass scattered in pools of rain water. The huge body of Dr. Yonas lying before him was an additional obstacle in his plan to get rid of Mariam Gatas. The worst thing was the threat that his leaking blood posed as it had polluted Jakov's hands and clothes.

"Blood is the worst trace that a Soft Angel could ever leave behind him at the crime scene."

Jakov remembered this rule that the Wolf of Sahoy had repeated to his team during their training. Blood, as a sticky liquid, makes it hard to protect the places where the crime has taken place. Blood is the first piece of evidence that catches the attention of the investigators, as it represents assured proof in linking its owner with the crime scene. A drop of blood is way worse than even fingerprints. The new technology of analyzing DNA allowed investigators, if they so pleased, to learn a lot of information from even the tiniest sample. They could identify the race of the owner of the blood, his skin colour, his genetic attributes, sometimes even his nationality or ethnicity. A drop of blood could draw up a complete composite sketch of its owner and provide new information in helping find him. In contrast, a fingerprint was not useful unless its owner had previous records in the police archives.

Jakov was thinking of all of this while imagining the potential ways he could get rid of Mariam. The orders he had received hadn't told him how to carry out the mission. It wasn't important how the death looked: whether it looked like suicide or a violent murder was secondary. The most important thing was that he was to avoid leaving mysterious clues and proofs that could provoke the investigators to pose more questions. The first scenario was to make Mariam appear as if she was a victim of greed. She had stolen an artefact from the discovery site. She had wanted this artefact all to herself, and so she had killed her colleague when they had disagreed on how to split the rewards. If the investigators were to find her body in an uninhabited area, like a desert, then they would believe that she had been involved with a mafia in smuggling artefacts. They would believe that she had been in over her head with them and they had killed her. But that scenario was no longer perfect as it had lots of obvious holes. First, this bear-sized human laying amongst a mess of broken glass complicated the story. Jakov had to improvise an extra scenario for a completely new crime. But first and foremost, he had to stop his bleeding. He would have to carefully make sure that there were no drops of blood left behind. There was a big chance that some of his blood had gotten on the victim's clothing. Fortunately the roof was wet and the falling rain would wash away any blood. The rain would aid in the elimination of any clues. Jakov walked around slowly, trying to avoid the shards of glass. He stopped at the entrance to Dr. Yonas' hut and wiped his feet carefully, making sure not to leave any prints on the dry floor inside. He started searching through the closets and looking through papers to try and find something to base his new scenario on. He needed to know something about the person he was about to kill.

*********

*Every night in my dreams*

*I see you. I feel you*

*That is how I know you go on.*

There is a very soft layer of cloud in which the consciousness dives between life and death. In this realm there is no existence of body, pain, or senses. For Mariam there was only the sound of Celine Dion coming from nowhere like a thin, transparent smoke. She didn't hear the music with her ears, yet she was aware of it somehow. In front of her eyes there was only darkness. She could not see. She was aware of the darkness but she also realized that there was a hidden light in it, like the glowing halos that surrounded the crowns of saints in old icons. She was aware of the same light that you could see in depictions of the holy mother's smile while she held the blessed infant. Could the kingdom of heaven be big enough to gather her and Ismail at the same time? Souls who are seeking salvation and spirits long for the heavens, and Mariam's heaven was in the heart of Ismail. Her hell was being denied him. Was the heaven of Muslims the same as the heaven of Christians? She was already cast out of her own paradise and so she had to find it between the ribs of Ismail - even if that paradise would be found in the depths of hell.

*Near, far, wherever you are*

*I believe that the heart does go on.*

Light was shining in front of her eyes but she could not see it. Something in her told her that this light was Ismail smiling for her. Then the light became stronger. It flowed through her and encompassed her being. She was aware of his words without hearing him - she had no ears and he had no lips.

"The mercy of God is endless and his own divine light shines on the whole universe in a way that doesn't leave a shred of darkness. The paradise of God is big enough for everybody who has but a glint of light in their hearts regardless of race or skin colour... It is only the paradise of religious people that reserves this glory for the followers while casting out all the rest. This false sanctity gives its blessing to whomever it chooses and curses everyone else."

*Once more you open the door*

*And you're here in my heart*

*And my heart will go on and on.*

The sound of the music grew louder, raising her upwards toward the heavens. She reached out with a hand that was not present and could feel the clouds passing through her fingers, washing them with tiny drops of rain. She could hear a man panting while she moved her head from side to side, and suddenly her soul was plunged into darkness again. She walked down a marble staircase and could hear her footsteps without seeing her feet moving. She entered into a cave and heard the moaning of a ferocious male cat. The sound of her footsteps quickened until they became small leaps. The taste of the pure rain drops had turned into mud. The light vanished and the music stopped. Death had disappeared. She felt cold. She opened her eyes. There was a hanging minaret between the land and sky.

✧✧✧✧✧✧✧✧✧

In spite of his panting, Joseph had managed to find a gap in the inner fence of the mosque of Ahmad. Lowering the precious load with complete care, he felt the cold air stabbing his lungs in viciously sharp breaths. He had exhausted himself from the great effort he had made in the last two minutes.

When Joseph had left to retrieve the laptop, he had stepped into the darkness of the tiny alleyway. He had only taken two steps when before him, walking towards him, there had appeared a thin ghost with an athletic build. He was heading towards the same dark doorway that Joseph had just exited. At first glance Joseph felt a strange chill when he saw the pale face heading towards him. The face bore the features of a foreigner who did not belong with the faces of the residents. In his hand there was a small device with a shining screen. He was peering into it. Slowing down his pace, Joseph looked at the man out of the corner of his eye as he passed by. He turned to see the ghost disappear into the darkness of the doorway.

The heart of Joseph sunk. It dawned on him how stupid they had been. The Blackberry that Mariam was carrying had enabled this mysterious ghost to follow them. After all, it was not her Blackberry. It had been sent to her through the chief editor. This meant that it was able to be programmed with a tracking feature.

Joseph turned around to follow the ghost and snuck through the darkness slowly. He returned to the doorway and entered the building. From downstairs he could not hear the steps of the ghost, but he saw a shadow that was hovering up the stairwell noiselessly. All of his suspicions were correct when he saw the ghost heading up towards the roof. Joseph followed on his tiptoes; his heart was beating as fast as the wings of a hummingbird. When he reached the entrance of the roof, Joseph peered out from the darkness of the stairwell onto a scene that made him panic. He saw Mariam lying on the roof at the feet of a panting man. Many thoughts ran through Joseph's mind at once. His immediate impulse was to attack the ghost, but he had never fought in his life before. If he lost the fight, then Mariam would lose any hope of rescue. When he saw how this mysterious man had knocked down the enormous Dr. Yonas with one foul blow, he had concluded that attacking the ghost would gain them nothing.

"Coward!"

The accusation appeared in his head. He was always taking the passive approach, always avoiding confrontations. Mariam had often joked with him about this in the cafeteria. Whenever the waiter had ripped him off or shortchanged him, he had paid with no fuss. She used to look at him with care in her eyes saying,

"Your heart is pure as white milk. Maybe if you had a few drops of South Egyptian blood in your veins, everything would be a lot better for you. I advise you to eat some hot peppers."

They had both laughed and his face had flushed. He knew she was right.

"I lost Mariam once before because I didn't tell her that I loved her. Then Ismail came and told her himself. He challenged everyone for her. I lost her once, but I will never lose her again - regardless of what happens."

A huge dose of adrenaline rushed through his blood and he responded to this sudden burst of determination. The man had entered the room of Dr. Yonas and had left the battlefield completely vacant. Joseph moved quickly and carefully. He looked around for any potential weapons on the roof, and found a piece of iron, less than a metre long. Maybe it was a piece of pipe that had been linked to the water deposit. With all of his might, he grasped the pipe and walked across the roof slowly. He avoided making any sound. If there was any chance of overcoming this monster, then his only hope would be the element of surprise. If he could just manage to hide behind the vines coming down from the roof of the hut... maybe this was his one chance. Maybe he could manage to get one blow in. Just one hard blow to the head... It would have to be one decisive, concentrated hit.

When he reached the vines, he was already beginning to pant from the excitement and thrill. Seeing Mariam lying there was paining his heart. He was unable to offer any help yet. She was unconscious, but by her rising and falling chest he could see that she was breathing. He peered through the crack in the door, trying to see what was going on inside Yonas' hut. Through the crack he could see a small part of a shoulder that must have belonged to the ghost. Joseph did not want to take any risks by attempting to get a better look. It was obvious that the ghost was searching the room for something.

As Celine Dion started to sing, Joseph realized that Mariam's cell phone was ringing. The moment to act was close, as this ghost would certainly try to silence the phone. In that moment all of the circumstances would be present and conditions would be ideal for that one, big hit. His grip tightened around the piece of iron and he readied his stance. His muscles contorted as he held his breath. He could feel the drops of sweat gathering on his forehead in spite of the cold air. Celine Dion continued to sing for another minute and then she went silent. Still, the ghost had not exited the hut. Joseph tried once again to peer through the crack in the door to see what was happening inside. At that moment he could see the ghost in his entirety. He was sitting on the old sofa on which Mariam had sat a few minutes ago. He opened the laptop and began to mess around with it.

"He must be deleting the pictures on the laptop," Joseph said to himself, trying to gather up some courage. He stretched out his neck slightly to extend his angle of vision. From the doorway the ghost could be seen in profile. He would have to turn his head a full 90 degrees to see Joseph at the doorway. Joseph thought that he could sneak past without catching the attention of the ghost and hit him from behind. But although the man might not see him, Joseph reasoned that he would definitely hear his footsteps. It was too risky. He shook off the idea immediately, losing hope in this scenario. His position in the darkness next to the door was his only advantage at this point.

Once again Celine Dion's singing on Mariam's phone caught the attention of Joseph. He looked carefully through the crack in the door and found the ghost still in his place in complete concentration. At that moment a daring idea dawned on Joseph. He craned his neck to look at the door itself. The hut's door opened from the outside and he noticed that the outer handle had the remains of an iron clasp. It seemed like this clasp had been used to lock the door when Yonas had left his room. In the doorframe there was a primitive hole that had been used to receive the bolt at one point. Joseph took a deep breath and immediately took action. He shoved the door closed and used the iron rod he was holding to lock the door. He quickly jammed it between the clasp and the hole in the frame, creating a makeshift lock. That was how he barricaded the ghost. He heard a mad curse come from inside the hut followed by fast steps and loud bangs. The loud bangs shook Joseph with fright, but the lock seemed resistant so far. He turned to look at Mariam and found her body lying very still. He didn't take a moment to think. Bending down to lift her onto his shoulders, he then ran towards the stairwell entrance while the wood of the hut's door was splintering under the silent blows of bullets. He managed to race down the steps keeping his balance with his precious load. A cat terrified him when it jumped through his legs in the darkness, and he almost fell. When he finally arrived outside he was panting and his legs and muscles felt like they were on fire. They were shaking and he could barely stand. Hearing the sound of steps descending down the stairwell, Joseph reacted quickly. Running towards the car was not an option as the ground was slippery from the rain and the vehicle was parked some distance away. Instead, he decided to head towards the fence of the Ahmad mosque which was only a few metres away. He approached the scaffolding left by the construction workers who were working to restore this ancient monumental building. When he ducked under the scaffolding he found a hole large enough for a body. The hole led to the north side of the mosque. He bent down a little and began climbing through the opening with Mariam on his shoulders. He heard her moan softly after she collided with a piece of wood that was sticking out of the scaffolding.

After a few metres, he found himself passing under one of a series of large archways. When he reached the open courtyard where before him stood the glorious ablution fountain, he felt as if he was going to collapse. He lowered Mariam gently to the ground and threw his exhausted body down beside her. He had made sure that they were hidden behind one of the pillars which comprised the base of the arches. He looked at Mariam's face. It was stained with mud. He met her eyes, which were smiling. Her gaze moved from him and climbed the minaret until it was lost in the sky.

*\*\*\*\*\*\*\*\*\**

Dr. Yahia Gatas had spent close to forty years in the operating room. Over time he had learned to control his temper. His talent as a surgeon supported by his ability to keep his emotions down and maintain his iron will had kept him calm when faced with the most difficult of situations. But when he took his first step into John Howard's office, he could not keep himself calm. His eyes spit fire at the professor, burning him. The grey haired man was sitting behind his huge desk with a dull look in his eyes. Despite the dim lighting, the desperate hours the professor had spent the previous night could be seen in his weary eyes. Dr. Yahia approached the desk and yelled in anger,

"The game is over, Professor. From now on, you will be solely responsible for my daughter's safety."

Professor Howard raised his head, trying to respond. For him the last sixty minutes had consisted of a terrible phone call that threatened to destroy his world as he knew it. The man standing in his office had managed in the last few hours to use his wide connections with politicians in Washington, scientists in Boston, and media officials in New York to throw Howard's entire life on the line. Even more dangerous than the connections of Yahia Gatas were the documents the surgeon had presented Howard with. He did not have a clue in hell what kind of devil had given Dr. Gatas this information, but before him lay the possibility of a terrible, international scandal that could destroy the reputations of many academic and political institutions in more than one location. Yahia had complete lists of everyone who was co-operating with the Sacred Historical Protocol.

"Please calm down, Dr. Gatas. Your daughter will be safe. The operation has been cancelled. I am waiting on a message from Cairo as we speak to let me know of her safety. I ask you just one thing..."

Yahia did not let the man finish his sentence.

"It is not your right to ask for anything. People like you do not deserve to live. There will be a day when you are called to answer for your crimes."

Professor Howard avoided the attack. He responded in a quiet, defeated voice,

"Dr. Gatas, you are a man of science. You know well that science sometimes needs to carry out actions that do not support our ethical conscience, but the aim is for a greater good. For example, you make life and death decisions in the operating room, and in genetic engineering labs and medical experiments there are lots of lives at stake. In return you know that millions of people rely on that research."

"That is stupid logic and a terrible comparison. We never hire murderers and criminals. You insult the honour of the academic profession."

"Dr. Gatas, my field is anthropology, a human science... If you say that surgeons and doctors deal with life and death on a daily basis, than it can be said that we deal with entire humanity on a much larger scale. Could you imagine the amount of chaos that could occur in societies if their foundations were touched? All of that knowledge... the facts that make up our realities... These pillars of religion, discipline, and sanctity give society its ethical stability. My vocation is to keep those pillars safe from any compromise."

The features of Dr. Yahia Gatas contorted into a grim smile.

"Your vocation?! Do you think that yourself and that group of hallucinating lunatics are carrying out vocations? Who are you to speak in the name of God? Who are you to claim the knowledge of truth for yourself? Who are you to enforce sanctity on only what you see is holy? The word of God is much stronger than you. It does not need to wait for people like you to prove its rights. The word of God is absolute reality. It is the light that ignites the heart. You are committing the worst sin of murder. It doesn't matter if you hide behind the masks of purification and sanctity, as the blood is still dripping from your hands."

Despite his exhausted features, Howard managed to pull a cunning smile across his face. He took a moment and said,

"You are saying this now because of personal reasons relating to your daughter. Your family history totally contradicts this emotional speech that you are delivering now."

A sudden surge of anger seized the soul of Dr. Gatas. For long decades and maybe even since the end of the nineteenth century, Dr.

Gatas' family in Egypt had been one of a few playing a very special and mysterious role. It gave them the power and fortune which they held to this day. Families like the Gatas' were playing the mediator role between numerous institutions and Western museums interested in artefacts and the treasure hunters of South Egypt, those simple minded people that might find pieces of gold, pottery, and scrolls of papyrus in their homes. This was a black market that passed through numerous complex paths and ended with specific families designated to mediate the trade of these goods between the simple minded groups of farmers that didn't understand the value of what they had discovered and the big institutions that had huge open budgets designated for collecting whatever might contradict the Sacred Historical Protocol. Thanks to the efforts of the mediators and their control of the market, the most important scrolls and manuscripts had leaked from Egypt to the museums and academic institutions of Europe and America as in the case of the scrolls of Nag Hammadi and the Gnostic Gospels. [4]

---

[4]  Nag Hammadi library is a collection of Gnostic texts discovered near the Upper Egyptian town of Nag Hammadi in 1945. Twelve leather-bound papyrus codices buried in a sealed jar were found by a local farmer named Muhammed al-Samman. The writings in these codices are comprised of fifty-two mostly Gnostic treatises, but they also include three works belonging to the Corpus Hermeticum and a partial translation/alteration of Plato's Republic. In his introduction to The Nag Hammadi Library in English, James Robinson suggests that these codices may have belonged to a nearby Pachomian monastery and were buried after Saint Athanasius condemned the use of non-canonical books in his Festal Letter of 367 A.D. The discovery of these texts significantly influenced modern scholarship into early Christianity and Gnosticism.

The contents of the codices were written in the Coptic language. The best-known of these works is probably the Gospel of Thomas, of which the Nag Hammadi codices contain the only complete text. After the discovery, scholars recognized that fragments of these sayings attributed to Jesus appeared in manuscripts discovered at Oxyrhynchus in 1898 (P. Oxy. 1), and matching quotations were recognized in other early Christian sources. Subsequently, a first or second century date of composition circa 80 AD or earlier has been proposed for the lost Greek originals of the Gospel of Thomas. The buried manuscripts date from the third and fourth centuries.

The Nag Hammadi codices are currently housed in the Coptic Museum in Cairo, Egypt.

The story of the discovery of the Nag Hammadi library in 1945 has been described as 'exciting as the contents of the find itself'. In December of that year, two Egyptian brothers found several papyri in a large earthenware vessel while digging for fertilizer around the Jabal al-Tarif caves near present-day Hamra Dom in Upper Egypt. Neither originally reported the find, as they sought to make money from the manuscripts by selling them individually at intervals. The brothers' mother burned several of the manuscripts, worried, apparently, that the papers might have 'dangerous effects' (Markschies, Gnosis, 48). As a result, what came to be known as the Nag Hammadi library (owing to the proximity of the find to Nag Hammadi, the nearest major settlement) appeared only gradually, and its significance went unacknowledged until sometime after its initial discovery.

In 1946, the brothers became involved in a feud, and left the manuscripts with a Coptic priest. The priest's brother-in-law in October that year sold a codex to the Coptic Museum in Old Cairo (this tract is today numbered Codex III in the collection). The resident Coptologist and religious historian Jean Doresse, realizing the significance of the artefact, published the first reference to it in 1948. Over the years, most of the tracts were passed by the priest to a Cypriot antiques dealer in Cairo, thereafter being retained by the Department of Antiquities, for fear that they would be sold out of the country. After the revolution in 1952, these texts were handed to the Coptic Museum in Cairo and were declared national property. Pahor Labib, the director of the Coptic Museum at that time, was keen to keep these manuscripts in their country of origin.

Meanwhile, a single codex had been sold in Cairo to a Belgian antique dealer. After an attempt was made to sell the codex in both New York and Paris, it was acquired by the Carl Gustav Jung Institute in Zurich in 1951 through the mediation of Gilles Quispel. The codex was intended as a birthday present to the famous psychologist; for this reason, this codex is typically known as the Jung Codex, being Codex I in the collection.

Jung's death in 1961 resulted in a quarrel over the ownership of the Jung Codex; the pages were not given to the Coptic Museum in Cairo until 1975 after a first edition of the text had been published. The papyri were finally brought together in Cairo: of the 1945 find, eleven complete books and fragments of two others, 'amounting to well over 1000 written pages' are preserved there.

"What you are saying is completely foolish. My family never killed anybody. My family worked with respectful academic institutions around the world, leading them to whatever was discovered. If it wasn't for their efforts, many scrolls would have been lost by falling in the wrong hands. Instead, they found care and scientific investigation. Besides, this practice that my family took part in was completely legal. In the past, trading monuments was not a crime. The Egyptians themselves dealt directly with academic intuitions, the same ones my family dealt with. Their goal was to preserve these artefacts and make sure that they were translated and studied."

"It doesn't matter. It is not important now if you try to justify your family's doings with a high noble aim. After all, the protocol strives for the same noble aim that is adopted by the biggest research institutions in the world. Hundreds of millions of dollars are spent every year to ensure that the ancient protocol is adhered to. If you condemn what I am doing now to protect the protocol, then you are contradicting yourself."

"Go to hell. You and your goddamned protocol. Are you claiming that you believe in God while at the same time you break his commandments?"

"It is not God who I believe in; it is Machiavelli. The end justifies the means. It is not important to believe in God. It is enough to believe in religion and the holy things that gather people and nations. If these holy things were violated, even if they are illusory, then the whole system on which human civilization has been built will collapse."

Dr. Yahia stared at the man who was addressing him while fighting back a burning rage. Dr. Howard was known in the American media as an opponent of anti-interventionism (the belief in one creator who does not intervene with his creation by any means), but he was also known in narrow academic circles as an atheist. Despite the American view of religion not being a subject for discussion, the idea that this atheist was saying was making Dr. Gatas sick. He tried to speak, but Professor Howard interrupted:

"This isn't the time to discuss religious beliefs. I'm not here to convince you of my logic, nor do I want to ask you to join the defenders of the Sacred Protocol. I know you are committed to keep your own secrets, and we have common friends - you can bet on that. From my side, I have cancelled the mission and very loyal followers will take care of everything in regards to your daughter. All I am asking from you is that your daughter commits to the same principle... that she gives her word in forgetting everything that has transpired within the last twenty-four hours."

"How could you ask this of her? Do you want her to just forget that a serious killer is after her? Do you want her to forget about the body in her apartment, and the clear threat of accusing her of murder in the first degree?"

In a glacial tone, Howard responded,

"Unfortunately the dead cannot be revived. Don't ask me to do what I could never do. Let us be practical. The apartment could be clear of the body and it would no longer have no relation with her. Accept my apology and my condolences and I will guarantee your daughter's safety."

Dr. Gatas took a deep breath. He was thinking about the series of phone calls and correspondences he had made before coming to this place. His scientific rank enabled him to have a wide source of connections that had allowed him to arrive at this deal that Howard was now offering him. Ironically, some of these common friends that Howard had spoken of were some of the best friends Dr. Gatas had ever had. Unfortunately it wasn't until this point that he had understood that they were part of the protocol. It is true that their hands were clean of any of the dirty work Howard had performed, this they had assured him, but they had also advised Yahia to make this deal in order to guarantee the safety of his daughter without compromising the protocol. Some had even used the same words that Howard had spoken in that cold glacial way, hiding a cold threat under the guise of sincere brotherly advice. Dr. Gatas knew this while listening to the offer Howard was making and he was fully ready to commit to the promise he had made to his friends. At the same time he was afraid of the reaction from his daughter that he had not seen in many years. He was afraid of her disobedience, especially since she knew all of his secrets.

"I am expecting everything to be over right now. The secrets of this goddamned protocol matter concern neither me nor my daughter," Dr. Gatas said. Then he turned and left the office, slamming the door behind him.

*\*\*\*\*\*\*\*\*\**

Howard let out a deep breath, finally feeling comfortable. The confrontation he had feared had been executed in a satisfying way. Over the course of history the protocol had faced many critical moments in which it could have collapsed along with its defenders, but as always everything seemed to be resolved for the better. Those responsible for protecting the protocol always managed to seize control once again. Dr. Howard closed his eyes to re-evaluate the whole situation: the violation that had occurred did not seem so serious. Dr. Gatas would never have dared to confront anyone so long as his daughter was safe. He had sent a message to Jacov Banshiev fifteen minutes ago to stop the operation at once and assure the safety of Mariam Gatas.

The buzzing of his Blackberry interrupted Howard's train of thought. He had been awaiting a response from the Soft Angel. When he read the message, he felt as if the earth was shifting under his feet.

"I am so sorry. This order has come too late. I have already lit my cigar."

"Holy Fuck!" Dr. Howard called out in a loud voice, seeing his whole world collapsing before him. The man who had just exited his office would now have nothing to stop him from avenging his daughter's death. There was only one option left. This was all according to the principles of the Sacred Protocol. His fingers shook typing away on his keyboard. There were desperate measures that needed to be taken. Then he stretched his hand out and opened his desk drawer. From it he pulled out an object that was as cold as it was shiny: a nine-millimetre pistol.

*-*-*-*-*-*-*

Outside of Professor Howard's office a touching and unique encounter was occurring between Dr. Gatas and Hannah Gabriel. The girl seemed to be the only survivor of a hurricane that had been manifested as a party in Beverly Hills. Her short backless dress was still adorning her beautiful body and her Dolce & Gabbana shoes were still sparkling on her feet, albeit her dress was a little dishevelled and her makeup had become spotty on her face. Under her eyes valleys had been carved into her foundation by tears. As much as her face was smiling at the sight of Dr. Gatas, her guilt-stained eyes spoke of a long night that she was not proud of. She was trying to avoid looking into his eyes directly. He couldn't see the appreciative look that in the past had given him such a warm feeling. In silence she approached the old doctor and he leaned forward to plant a fatherly kiss on her forehead. She started crying.

"Thank you, daughter, I will never forget what you have done for me."

Hannah had just written her resignation letter on the computer. When she raised her eyes to look up at the doctor, she felt confusion. It was her who owed him everything.

"Do you have any news about Mariam? Did you check in with her?"

"Don't worry, my dear. Everything will be fine thanks to you. The documents and information you sent to me worked like magic. They didn't just save my daughter; they assured me now that even if I am in my grave I will be able to cause the biggest scandal in history."

With a dramatic gesture he bowed and motioned to the car.

"Now, my young lady, as you need a ride, I have a car."

Hannah smiled while she took his hand and walked with him down the corridor. She was in dire need of a shower where she could rid herself of this clown-like face she was wearing. When both of them reached the main exit of the building, Dr. Gatas' car was waiting at the bottom of the marble stairs leading to the sidewalk. From the moment they hit the first stair they heard the sound of a condensed gunshot coming from somewhere inside. The bullet had left the chamber and could not be stopped.

*\*\*\*\*\*\*\*\*\**

Small pieces of splintered wood flew across the roof of Dr. Yonas and rained down on the man's large body. The rain was falling tremendously and the doctor was trying to move his face away from the pool of water that had gathered under his right cheek. He couldn't move his head, but through his peripheral vision he could see that the door of his hut was being shattered by a hail of bullets. From behind the debris came a human monster that cursed in a loud voice. Dr. Yonas felt his heart leap from his chest as he watched the boots of the monster approach him. The monster grabbed the back of his neck with iron claws and he felt a very light sting on the roof of his mouth. Darkness began to consume the old doctor.

Jakov Banshiev had decided that the mission had to be done. He didn't understand how the girl could have returned to consciousness and escaped.

"Stubborn bitch," he murmured under his breath as he checked his nose and found it swollen from the blow. He still had the remains of that last encounter on his shirt. Despite his instructions to cancel the mission, the girl had seen his face; this was a hard line in the work of the Soft Angels. This would be the end of his professional life. There was no room for coincidence or hesitating about orders that had come too late.

The Soft Angel had left his victim dying in silence and moved swiftly and quietly away. He longed to light his cigar and knew that his next victim would be worth it.

*\*\*\*\*\*\*\*\*

"Mariam! Mariam!"

The sound of Joseph's cries had penetrated the doors of her perception and the haze of unconsciousness dissipated. Her look climbed down from the sky and fixed on the face of a very worried Joseph. Her lips began to move as she tried to pronounce his name,

"Joseph ..."

She heard her voice coming up from inside her without feeling her lips. Her voice sounded as if it was a mysterious echo in an old Pharaonic temple. The walls in this temple were high and the stone columns were heightened in this atmosphere. She remembered what had transpired on the roof a few moments prior. She tried desperately to smile. Joseph embraced her with care while trying to wipe the dirt and grime that had gathered on her forehead.

"Where are we now?"

"We are in the Mosque of Ahmad ben tolon. I couldn't make it to the car; that man is still chasing us. Your dad called a few minutes ago from Boston and I told him you were safe."

She felt her blood boiling and she woke up completely to find herself yelling in anger:

"My father?! My father!? What the hell does he want and why the hell did you respond to him? How did he know I was in danger?"

"This is no time to be angry. Your dad is trying hard to get us out of this mess. You must know now that he is totally innocent of Ismail's murder."

"Did you actually believe him? You just don't... my dad..."

"It's not important what you believe right now. There are too many things you don't know at this time. Your dad will call us back in a few minutes when he makes sure the danger is gone. He will find us a way out of this." Joseph fell silent for a moment and then added, "You won't believe this, but the murderer of Ismail may be the same man who is after you now. Can you move?"

Mariam felt like her brain was as paralyzed as her body. What Joseph had said didn't seem logical or coherent to her. She tried to move her hands and legs and could hardly manage. She still felt like they were tied down. She tried to respond to Joseph but she felt as if her brain was also tied down in this fashion. She heard Joseph gasp in horror while he glanced at the southern corridor of the mosque. Then his next words were cut off by the thunder coming from the sky. In the distance the lightning revealed the silhouette of a ghost moving in silence through the giant puddles that covered the whole of the courtyard. The man was looking at something that was giving off a faint glow in his right hand while in his other hand there was a gun.

"He found us," Joseph whispered to her while his hands were searching her coat. He pulled out the Blackberry she had been given. Once again, the thunder had struck.

"We can't make it out this way. Stay where you are; he won't find you in this darkness. I will try to mislead him."

Her objection vanished under the crash of thunder and he didn't wait for her response. He took the Blackberry and ran away through the northern corridor while hiding behind the huge columns. He headed toward the twisted minaret. The eyes of Mariam were frozen in a stare when she saw the ghost cross the open courtyard in Joseph's direction.

\*\*\*\*\*\*\*\*\*\*

In the year 879 AD the Muslim governor Ahmad Ben Tolon had inaugurated the great mosque that bore his name. This mosque had been built by a Coptic engineer called Sayeed Ben Katup, and was considered the most ancient and monumental in Cairo. Its unique minaret was considered the most outstanding and lavish in the city of a thousand minarets. There was no other minaret like it except in the mosque of Samarra in Iraq. It was distinguished by its external spiral staircase with a width of about 150 centimetres revolving around the tower until it reached the top. It was said that the unusual shape of this minaret was designed by pure chance when the governor Ahmad Ben Tolon was sitting around playing with a piece of paper. After a moment he found that he had wound the paper into a spiral. He loved the design and instructed the architect to construct it in such a fashion, saying, "I want the minaret to be of this shape." It was speculated that he was worried that he had wasted the time of his people by playing with the paper, and so had claimed that this had been his intention the whole time.

Joseph was thinking about this old story that he had mentioned in one of his reports a few weeks ago. He had never imagined then that his life could be decided by the information he had gathered for the report. He arrived at the northern corridor of the mosque and entered the rain-soaked courtyard. He knew where he needed to step to begin the climb up the minaret, and there he could hide the Blackberry amongst the scaffolding that the restoration workers had used. Perhaps he could even throw it onto one of the roofs of the neighbouring houses in order to mislead this hired ghost without putting Mariam in harm's way.

Joseph began to climb the staircase but after a few steps he slipped and lost his balance. The staircase was covered in rain. The stairs had also been built with a slight tilt to the outside in order to prevent the rain from gathering there. And as much as this design was useful to keep the stairs clear of water erosion, it made it very difficult to climb to the top. One had to be very careful as there was no railing for support. This was the reason why the Egyptian Supreme Council of Antiquities had banned tourists from climbing the minaret - even though the view from the top was beautiful. Sometimes tourists went as far as to bribe the guards on duty to let them up.

Joseph had managed to make two revolutions around the tower on his way up by clinging to the stone wall. He had made it halfway up when he looked into the open courtyard to see the pale ghost advancing towards him much faster than he had imagined. The ghost had crossed the courtyard and was now at the base of the ancient tower. At that moment lightning had struck to reveal the face of the murderer staring up at Joseph with a look of frightening ferocity.

The pale ghost had managed to locate him and he had blocked any chance of escape. There was no option other than jumping from a height of about 40 metres, which was the halfway point, or continuing the climb upwards to buy some more time.

Jakov Banshiev was not in a hurry to chase his victim. The GPS had spotted the victim on the top of the minaret. He had also figured out the height she had reached so far, as when the lightning had lit up his surroundings he had spotted a human figure trying to hide from him by leaning on the inner wall about halfway up.

"Mariam Gatas is trapped. I finally got her."

This is what Jakov thought to himself as he put away the Blackberry. He felt the Cuban cigar in his pocket that was waiting for him. There was no need to rush. She had trapped herself and there was no way out. He took his time climbing the wet stairs with caution. As he climbed, he was imagining various scenarios in his head. He would not underestimate the woman a second time, because she had already proven herself to be more than competent. She might now be equipped with some sort of primitive weapon and be taking advantage of having control from her vantage point at the top. He placed his back against the inner wall of the minaret and continued up, using the darkened screen of his Blackberry as a mirror so that he could see around the curves ahead. He was careful to keep his footing and was ready for any surprise that Mariam might throw in his direction.

A sudden wave of fear had seized Mariam Gatas as she watched the ghost moving in the same direction that Joseph had gone. He was moving towards the minaret with noticeable speed. She tried hard to get to her feet by using the stone pillars as a crutch. She had regained control of all of her senses, but she still felt great pain throughout her body. On the back of her head there was blood from hitting the floor after the ghost had shocked her with his taser. With stumbling steps she limped towards the minaret, and when she entered the open courtyard the cool rain woke her completely. She surrendered to the rain. She raised her head up and received the water with welcome as it shocked her into attention. The minaret looked like the crow's nest of a ship in the middle of an ocean storm. She moved towards it. It had been closed off for construction but access to the staircase was still available. Her legs were still wobbly, but with an iron will she managed to persevere.

*************

Climbing the minaret became harder and harder with every curve of the spiral. The force of the wind was getting stronger the closer Joseph came to the top. He felt the bitter cold penetrating his bones and it shook him inside. For Jakov the training in the cruel Siberian winter had made him immune to anything that was any less cold. The only thing that the Soft Angel cared about was the speed of the wind, because this force could potentially increase the risk of falling from these narrow steps. He was extremely careful because he knew that his victim was like a cornered rat: even though it was small and appeared harmless, it could be extremely vicious in its last moments. He had to be prepared for any possible sudden movements. That was why he was mindful of his footing and made sure the left temple of his head was flush with the stone wall.

On the other side Mariam was crawling on all fours, because she had found that when she stood she stumbled. She continued climbing while murmuring to herself in a low voice,

"Our father who art in Heaven,

Hallowed be thy name,

Thy Kingdom come,

Thy Will be done on earth as it is in Heaven."

She was reciting her final prayer in her realization that she was crawling like an animal to her death. She did not feel afraid. Rather, there was a different feeling - a strange feeling of curiosity and surprise. She wished that she could reach Joseph before the murderer just so he could explain to her the sentence he had uttered in the middle of a thunder crash:

"The murderer of Ismail could be the same man who is after you now..."

Joseph had offered this suggestion and left her a victim of confusion.

Before the final spiral in the minaret, Jakov took a deep breath and filled his lungs with the cold air. He was almost at the top, which consisted of a tiny domed room. This room was dedicated for "Moazen", the one responsible for calling out the prayer. This room was the victim's last shelter. He adjusted his body so that he faced the entrance of the room. At the top there awaited a narrow staircase. However, his turn had brought with it an unexpected surprise. There behind him was something climbing on the lower third of the tower. Under the flashes of light it appeared that the figure was none other than Mariam crawling on her hands and knees. How the hell could this bitch manage to have misled him and now be coming from behind? The staircase was the only way to go up or down.

"She must have climbed down the scaffolding," Jakov thought to himself while he examined the scaffolding surrounding the upper part of the minaret... She might have had to make a desperate acrobatic jump, but it was for certain her only option. Jakov wouldn't need to risk running down the staircase to catch her. He could easily hit her from his current position. In complete silence the Soft Angel aimed his gun at the girl who was unaware of the death that was coming from above. The sound of the silenced bullet accompanied by a guttural shout was lost under the crash of thunder that came from the sky.

*************

A few employees of the institute had gathered at the sound of the gun shot. Dr. Gatas and Hannah were running quickly towards the commotion, and when everyone had arrived they were faced with a horrible sight. There was Howard with blood pouring from his mouth and his eyes were frozen in a dead stare. Blood was splattered across the curtains behind him caused by the exit wound. His hand was wrapped around the butt of a nine-millimetre pistol, which the investigator later confirmed he had owned for a long time.

*❊❊❊❊❊❊❊❊❊❊*

The body of Mariam shrank in pain when she received a scorching hot bullet through her upper torso. She thought that she saw a ghost fall past her towards the cold, cold ground. As she tried to pull herself to the edge of the step in order to look down, she found the body of the ghost that had attacked her a few minutes ago laying in a contorted position on the ground at the base of the minaret. His head had been totally smashed on the stones which had been left behind by the workers. When she looked up at the top towards the minaret, she saw the face of Joseph looking down at her from the upper part of the minaret. She was unable to make out his facial expression in the darkness, but she felt as if he was smiling in triumph. She smiled in return and she imagined that he could feel her smile as well, even if he couldn't see her. Her breath was hot and there was the metallic taste of blood in her mouth. Before she surrendered to the darkness, she heard the sound of Celine Dion singing,

"And my heart will go on and on."

*❊❊❊❊❊❊❊❊❊❊*

The next morning Mariam awoke to a bright white light surrounding her. Behind the window, the winter sun was shining in declaration of its victory against the storm that had rained down on Cairo over the past two days. The sky was clear except for a few tiny clouds that looked like little sheep walking across the river of the empyrean. She tried to raise herself but was immediately attacked by pain. Her arm was connected to an IV. She moaned in a loud voice to find Joseph coming towards her. He said "Good Morning" while his tired eyes smiled at her. The doctor had managed to remove the bullet that had gone through her left lung. Fortunately the bullet had missed the heart by a few centimetres without injuring the spinal column in any way. She had been rushed to hospital shortly after the showdown in the tower.

"The investigators are arriving soon. In the official police statement I said that we were attacked by a thief and you were shot during the fight."

Mariam looked at him with interrogating eyes, but he continued on with a hint of sadness:

"Nothing we learned last night can be revealed in your statement. This is what your dad had arranged in his deal. Remember the murder of Isaak Shuaib inside your own apartment? Your dad did his best using all his connections to close this matter and remove the dead body."

"But how could we just ignore the murder of our workmate?"

"Unfortunately, Mariam, we have no other choice; it's too much for us to find. Isaak will not be the first journalist to disappear in mysterious circumstances without his body ever being found.[5] He will certainly not be the last. And anyway, the justice of heaven has been achieved one way or another: the murderer has been killed."

Then Joseph showed her the third edition of the institution pointing to a small title at the corner of the page of the criminal news:

**A Russian tourist was killed while trying to climb the minaret of Ahmad Ben tolon mosque.**

And next to the news there was an official picture that seemed to have been taken off a passport showing the thin face of the blond man that Mariam had fought on the roof of Dr. Yonas's house. Then Joseph pointed out the details of the news report, saying, "Do you know that they believe that he died a few minutes after sunrise? They reported that he was a tourist who wanted to take pictures of the sunrise from the top of tolon mosque when he suddenly fell off the minaret. Although you and I know he was armed when we met him, the official police report never mentions any details about the possession of weapons. We cannot know who came at night to clean up the crime scene, put a camera in his hand instead of the pistol, and cut any ties between this assassin and the organization that hired him. Surely they are the same people that got rid of the dead body of Isaak Shoaib in your apartment. Obviously the protocol of the holy history has agents that are spread out all over the world."

---

[5] The disappearance of journalists or activists in Egypt may occur without any explanation. On the 11th of August, 2003 Reda Helal the Egyptian journalist and the deputy editor of AL-AHRAM newspaper disappeared and was never found. Reda is the most famous case of this kind because he was a high ranking journalist, but he represents a lot more young journalists and activists who have been exposed to enforced disappearances and were never seen again.

Mariam seemed unconvinced. A nurse came to check her vitals and inject her I.V. with a drug prescribed by the doctor. The nurse said that this drug would help her to sleep. As her mind started to swim in a white cloud of fog, she heard Joseph asking her to stop talking and rest. But she stretched out her hand to grab hold of Joseph:

"Dad, Ismail, what do they have to do with all this? Please don't leave me."

Joseph held her hand kindly. He waited until the nurse had left, and then he whispered in her ear:

"Mariam, your dad never killed Ismail; I'm sure of this."

Mariam heard Joseph's voice coming from a faraway place as if she was in a deep well. She closed her eyes and saw herself drowning in mud and rain. She was lying on the stone stairs and then her cell phone rang... she heard her dad's voice calling her from faraway... Joseph came to tear apart his shirt to stop her bleeding and she could hear the angels singing in their beautiful voices that overcame the thunder's sound.

Over the following days Mariam learned all of the hidden details of the painful story of Ismail. In bits and pieces whenever she could stay awake she found out all of the scattered parts of the whole story.

Through brief phone calls with her dad in Boston, documents and other information that came through her email, and the kind smile of Joseph who watched over her day and night, she found herself finally gathering together the scattered lines and pieces of information to form the story that had changed the course of her life.

Ismail had been studying in London in preparation for his PhD thesis in microbiology. During this time Ismail was researching a few Egyptian mummies that were resting in the museum of Flinders Petrie. Sir William Flinders Petrie, who lived from 1853 and 1942, was a pioneer British Egyptologist and the first to set the rules of Egyptology in British universities. He was committed to the necessity of connecting all archaeological discoveries with the holy book. With this purpose in mind, he excavated many archeological sites in Egypt and in southwest Palestine in 1933. When he retired, Petrie moved to Jerusalem where he lived with his wife in the British school of archeology and worked temporarily in the American School of Eastern Research. His personal belongings and collections that he had acquired throughout his excavations formed the basis of a huge museum in London that contained 80000 pieces.

Ismail's study focused on analyzing the micro-organisms that existed in the tissues of the Egyptian mummies in order to calculate the exact time and date of the mummification. These studies seemed to worry those who were responsible for the protocol of the holy history. If the timeline of the micro-organisms contradicted with the given history of the mummies, this would surely push back the history of those mummies to make them thousands of years older than they were supposed to be. The medical technology that Ismail used could have caused a revolution in Egyptology by rewriting history in a way that contradicted the rule of thumb previously set forth by the keepers and the pioneers of the protocol of holy history. To Ismail's misfortune, the ancient protocol had started a new wave of violence ever since the Neo-conservative parties had started to take control in many countries of the Western world. When politics married religion, both became more violent and dangerous.

"Do you remember a professor in medical school called Saeed Thabit?"

Once again, Mariam navigated back through many years in her memory to a time when she was a student visiting South Egypt. As part of a larger group of university students, they had visited the temple of Dendara. Dr. Saeed Thabit was the head of the committee of history lovers at the faculty of medicine and the supervisor of this excursion.

Ismail Alkhazindar, as Dr. Saeed's teacher assistant, had a deep and long lasting friendship with this professor. Dr. Saeed Thabit later published a theory about the Pharaoh of Exodus. This theory stated that that all the details of the Exodus should have happened in the Predynastic Period; in other words, the story belonged to the prehistoric era before Egyptians started to use writing to register events. Thus, the story had been transferred orally amongst generations to become the myth of Osiris.

The myth of Osiris was the oldest myth in the ancient Egyptian civilization. Its details reached back to the prehistoric era. Osiris was a king of Egypt who was murdered by his brother Seth. Seth had put Osiris into a coffin and thrown him in the Nile River. Osiris's wife searched for his body. When she finally found it, she sat beside it crying until the gods helped her to conceive a son from her dead husband. She gave birth to Horus, who would later take revenge upon his uncle Seth.

The theory supposed that Osiris was the embodiment of the struggle between Moses and Pharaoh. The priest of Egypt denied the defeat of their king against a bunch of foreigners by changing the story in a way that glorified their king against his enemies. Then Moses turned into Seth, the evil brother who conspired to kill his brother, and Pharaoh turned into Osiris who would eventually win by his son taking revenge in his name. Osiris became the king of the underworld, and this was a form of a victory for him.

This theory justified the word "pharaoh" which was mentioned in all the holy books. It had been stated that the word pharaoh was never a title, but it was the exact name of that king. Dr. Saeed said that this king had a name that was linked to the word own (or iwn) which is the Holy City of Sun (nfr-iwn). In the ancient Egyptian language this name means "the beautiful of the city of Iwn". This word was converted by the Semitic languages like Hebrew and Arabic to the word "pharaoh".

Many Egyptologists disagreed with this theory that Dr. Saeed published in his book entitled *Who Is The Pharaoh of Exodus?* The main reason the Egyptologists disagreed with the theory was because Dr. Saeed was not an Egyptologist who was specialized in ancient Egyptian history. They did not even care to discuss the details of the theory in a scientific way to prove if it was correct or not.

"But why did Dr. Saeed not face the same destiny as Ismail?" asked Mariam bitterly.

Joseph reminded her with the words that Dr. Yonas had said to them on the roof of his house on that rainy night: "As a matter of fact, not all researchers of ancient history are facing dangers; many of them are merely adventurers looking for fame without even having any academic credibility. These kind of researchers would never threaten the protocol. Their theories are so easy to criticize because they are not specialists, and so they are dealt with as clowns. The same thing happens to the researchers of UFOs or to those who have formed theories about the construction of the pyramids by aliens. This kind of research could never threaten the mainstream academic research of history and archeology. So that's how they dealt with the theory of the Pharaoh of Exodus. Only serious researchers with academic credibility and specialized studies that could affect the principles of mainstream historic studies could pose a real threat to the protocol. Only in this case could it turn into a real serious matter where interference with the protocol keepers would be inevitable.

"The studies of Ismail seemed to threaten the protocol keepers. They felt the danger of the credibility of Ismail and decided to stop him, especially when they learned about the relationship between him and Dr. Saeed Thabit. They did not believe it was a coincidence for a researcher like Ismail to be in the middle of the Petrie museum in London researching and investigating evidence in connection with the founder of the theory of the Pharaoh of Exodus. At first they tried to influence the results of Ismail's research by limiting the funding, redirecting the research to other various points of interest, or putting academic barriers in his way to cause delay. In the end, Professor John Howard made the violent decision to get rid of Ismail via murder. Two years later when Professor John Howard found out that the young widow of Ismail had confronted the police and broke through the red line of the restricted area to take pictures of an important archeological discovery, not wanting to take any chances he had suddenly made another violent decision to murder Mariam. He would prevent the publishing of any pictures that could open the locked doors of the forgotten City of the Sun."

"Does the timeline of the ancient Egyptian civilization deserve all this damn blood? Does it deserve all these murders and crimes to hide it?" Mariam asked, panting as she tried to comprehend the massive flow of information flooding her fainting consciousness.

Joseph answered her by reading some documents that had been sent by Dr. Yahia Gatas over the internet:

"We are now in the year 2015 and we all know that this calendar that we use started with the birth of Christ. In the Islamic calendar we have passed the year 1430 and we all know that the zero point of this calendar is the migration of the prophet Muhammad from Mecca to Al-Medina. But what about the Jewish calendar? We are now in the year 5770 according to the Hebrew calendar. What would be the point zero in that calendar? The Jewish scholars say that the point zero of the calendar is the creation of earth, but this has been proven to be mistaken. Point zero of the calendar should rather be the date of Exodus. By this calculation Exodus would be older than the age of King Narmer, the first king in Egyptian history. This theory would move the ancient history of Egypt back thousands of years in contradiction with the history that has been proven by the protocol. The studies carried out by Ismail were going to present enough proof to reread and rewrite history differently than all the holy books."

With every dose of drugs, antibiotics, and pain killers that relieved her from the pain came a surge of information and details that helped answer all the questions she had in her head. Every now and then she would slip back into unconsciousness only to wake up to another dose of medicine and another piece of information to complete the puzzle.

Mariam listened to her father's voice coming from Boston over the phone. She felt his pain and regret for what had happened to Ismail.

"He was a real man; he tried always to have me forgive you, but I was stubborn and stupid. I'm so proud of your choice, my dear daughter, and I do bless your marriage even if it's too late. I hope you believe that I will never repeat that mistake again." The last sentence was spoken by Dr. Yahia Gatas in a mysterious way that Mariam did not understand.

*-*-*-*-*-*-*-*-*

A few days later she was surprised by her kids Adam and Sarah visiting with her mother-in-law who spoke to her with unexpected kindness. When she asked Joseph later about the surprising change in her mother-in-law's attitude toward her, he responded, smiling,

"My aunt finally calmed down when she understood that her foreigner daughter-in-law will never kidnap her grandchildren and take them away to the USA. She now knows that her daughter-in-law is going to marry a good man who will be able to take care of her and control her at the same time."

Mariam laughed at Joseph saying the last sentence as if he was an actor on the stage before an audience, and then she responded arrogantly:

"That easy! Without even asking for her acceptance. I have already told you I will look into your request and study it. Later I will decide whether or not to accept."

"First, it's an offer you can never refuse: I saved your life, and it is now my right to marry you."

"And second?.........."

"Second, you come from a South Egyptian family, and in your culture girls have no right to refuse a proposal that has been accepted by their parents."

Worrying about her dad's opinion, she had postponed thinking of Joseph's proposal. She didn't want to undergo this painful discussion with her dad once again.

"Really? Did you talk to him? Did he accept?" asked Mariam in surprise.

"Sure he accepted; how could he find for his daughter a better man than me? He will come all the way from America tomorrow morning to complete the procedures of our marriage before the Christmas holidays."

Over the next days and weeks journals and magazines published scattered news reports which none of the readers or even editors could have imagined were linked in any way. For example,

**The Egyptian surgeon Dr. Yahia Gatas comes back to Cairo for the first time in ten years**

**The search for the missing journalist Isaak Shoaib continues; police confirm no criminal suspects**

**According to Wiki, new documents are being prepared that may cause a huge academic and political scandal**

**Mansi Abd-Allah is chosen to be the new Minister of Media**

**Famous Egyptologist Dr. Yonas Idris is rescued after a drug overdose**

The official website of UNISCO has been hacked by anonymous hackers who replaced the symbol of the organization with the symbol of the City of Sun (Nfr Iwn)

Finally, THE SPHINX's community page presented the following headline accompanied by a large photograph:

**Congratulations to our colleagues Joseph Alnagar and Mariam Gatas on their marriage.**